Titles I

The Wages of Corruption

Sammy Oke Akombi

Langaa Research & Publishing CIG
Mankon, Bamenda

Publisher:
Langaa RPCIG
Langaa Research & Publishing Common Initiative Group
P.O. Box 902 Mankon
Bamenda
North West Region
Cameroon
Langaagrp@gmail.com
www.langaa-rpcig.net

Distributed outside N. America by African Books Collective
orders@africanbookscollective.com
www.africanbookscollective.com

Distributed in N. America by Michigan State University Press
msupress@msu.edu
www.msupress.msu.edu

ISBN: 9956-558-47-8

DISCLAIMER

The names, characters, places and incidents in this book are either the product of the author's imagination or are used fictitiously. Accordingly, any resemblance to actual persons, living or dead, events, or locales is entirely one of incredible coincidence.

Contents

The most ignoble prison
For transparency
Is corruption.

Preface

After establishing the credibility of Transparency International, who twice have accorded our country the infamous first place in corruption, true patriots were moved and they realised that something was in fact wrong somewhere and something had to be done somehow. Cameroonians in one voice thought they should wage a war against this 'most unusual friend of fairness.'

By way of tackling the issue, I thought I should elicit awareness through the short story. The first in this collection *The Politician* is on politics and about the politician. This is not by accident because 'man' in Aristotle's opinion 'is by nature a political animal.' Also, our governance is wholly controlled by politicians and I was inspired by the fact that there is so much corruption in our politics that if we allow it to persist, we risk handing to posterity a nation:

In which it will be common place to punish people according to the politics they champion rather than the laws they violate or the personal misconduct in which they engage. We will in short become a nation of men and not of laws. W.J. Bennett

The second story *The Sacrificed Lunch Pack* is on education and about Alice, a typical school pupil in our country. There is this saying that goes: 'show me your friend and I'll tell you what you are.' I would like to develop it thus: 'show me your passport and I'll tell you what you are.' Education cultivates the citizenry. It builds in the individual a certain confidence, nobility, probity, sobriety and integrity. If our education must produce individuals with such sterling qualities then it must be rid of corruption. It must be managed by people who themselves possess the qualities that we expect from the youngsters.

The rest of the stories are on corruption in different segments of society in our country and about the people who perpetrate it. We all are immersed in it and so must make every effort to resurface from it. It takes only the will to stay alive because the wages of corruption like any other sin can only be death.

I would like to acknowledge that these stories have been broadcast on CRTV Buea in the programme *the English you speak*, produced by the Southwest Regional Linguistic Centre, Buea. Also many thanks to the Rt. Rev. Dr. Nyansako Ni-Nku, Moderator of the Presbyterian Church in Cameroon for readily accepting to write the foreword of this book.

Sammy Oke Akombi
Buea, 25th May 2009

Foreword

I have had the pleasure of reading through the manuscript of this piece. I find that it is an exciting collection of stories brilliantly narrated by Sammy Oke Akombi, on some burning issues of societal morality. The first story *The Politician*, explores the place of the politician in Cameroon today and their role in the domain of good governance. The other story that particularly caught my interest is *The Sacrificed Lunch pack*. It touches on corruption in the realm of education.

The issues of governance and corruption are permanent on the agenda for discussion where two or three Cameroonians congregate. We all have our models of what the perfect society should be and how the genuine public servant should perform. In this work Sammy Oke Akombi has made an invaluable contribution to that national debate.

In our search for the good in our society and ourselves, we realize that human value is decreasing in our country so that even heinous crimes like murder, which before was an abomination in traditional society, have now become mere sport for some people. In the process, impunity has taken centre stage in our contemporary culture.

The moral lesson conveyed here is strong. When shall Cameroonians be humans again? When shall we learn the age old truth that we were designed to be one another's keeper? And that this will be possible only when we have a cleaner, saner and morally healthier community of decent people. Or is that too utopian?

RT. REV. Dr. NYANSAKO NI-NKU
Moderator of Presbyterian Church in Cameroon (PCC) and former President All African Conference of Churches (AACC)
Buea, 20th June 2009.

The Politician

There was an impending election and there was a politician, candidate for the lone parliamentary seat for Griefland constituency. The candidate and his aides developed and adopted a strategy. It was to pocket all the village heads of this constituency. He was not going to pocket them with dependable ideas and laudable plans for the people. It was with pieces of gold, thirty pieces for each village head. The politician succeeded to have all of them, thirty in number, in his pocket. One of the village heads, very enthusiastic about his throne, and having a vainglorious opinion of himself, got everyone to know him as, and address him as His Royal Highness, Chief Nfor Seseku Nyukechen the first of Tarkamanda.

Chief Nyukechen had displayed so much zeal in the politician's campaign that note was easily taken of him. He had assured the politician of his total loyalty and that of the people of Tarkamanda. On the eve of the election he had convened a meeting of all his people and instructed them on the appropriate pattern of voting. Moreover, he requested them to swear by the gods of the ancestors of the land that his instructions were obeyed. A day after the election, the results for Griefland constituency were announced and the politician won with an impeccable majority of 70%. His strategy had worked wonderfully well. But chief Nyukechen was very unhappy. He had promised the politician 100% but Tarkamanda had scored 99.99%. This had not gone down well with the chief. He was bent on fishing out those black legs who had deprived him of the total fulfilment of his promise to the politician. He

1

wanted to punish them severely for failing to adhere to the instructions of his royal highness. He requested the electoral officials to give him the ballot papers of those who had voted against the politician in order for him to identify them. But they told him it was unnecessary because this time around, politics had evolved towards a democracy, which should not allow for vindictiveness and besides, the choice candidate had won. The politician had to assure him that he had been very grateful for the service he had rendered and he should wait and see what he had for the Tarkamanda people in particular and the Griefland constituency as a whole.

The politician took his honourable seat in the assembly and among his gains in parliament was a generous annual parliamentary grant for micro projects in the constituency. At the end of the session the politician went home with pockets full. He intimated Chief Nyukechen about his plans for the grant. They quickly agreed on a town hall project which would be financed by the grant and contributions from the elite of Tarkamanda. The project manager was HRH Chief Nyukechen himself. The following day, the people were gathered and told about the project and they all hailed their chief and the politician. And on the spot, a sum of two million CFA francs was raised by the elite. In addition, letters were prepared for and sent to each member of the Tarukamanda elite, appealing for more financial support for the project.

At the end of the second year after the launching of the project, the elite of Tarkamanda had noticed not even a skeletal shadow of the project. So they met to assess what was going on. But the project manager, who was the able royal highness himself, was everything but cooperative.

All he was persuaded to show was a thousand moulded blocks which had been carefully packed at a corner in the royal palace. His royal highness refused to hand in any records for proper accounting. Apart from, the on-the-spot contribution of two million francs, some members of the elite had also sent sums of money to the project manager and they wanted to know how he had spent it or intended to spend it.

His royal highness could not produce any records on the amount of money he had received, so far. Fortunately, he had responded positively to the invitation to attend the meeting which had been called by the elite. The politician too had been invited.

Shortly after the meeting had begun, the spokesperson for the elite took the floor,

"Your honour, honourable member of parliament, you remember two years ago you raised the hopes of the Tarkamanda village, when you launched the town hall project. You might have noticed that we were all happiness and enthusiasm and on the spot we raised a handsome sum towards the project. Besides, some other members of the elite had sent huge sums of money to his royal highness, the project manager. You, on your part had pledged fifty percent of the annual parliamentary grant to the project, for the four years following. Could we know how much of this money had been handed to the project manager, so far?"

The politician stood up and cleared his throat but before he could say anything, his royal highness stormed out of his seat, "You rat, what right! What right have you got to ask the honourable gentleman about the way he spends his money, eh you scallywag? Come to think of it, these so - called elite are people who come to the village only once in a blue moon. What do they think they are and what do they know about Tarkamanda?"

The politician was visibly taken aback by the reaction of his royal highness. He had stood up to say something but the boisterous chief had not given him a chance. He simply stood where he was, completely rattled. His royal highness rescued him as he walked up to him and grabbed him awkwardly by the hand saying, "Let's get out of here. Since when had rats and despicable gnats like these started to embarrass their superiors. They must be demon-crazy."

The politician was not very sure of the stance to take but he could not help going along with his royal highness. The chief had been one of his chief strategist during the elections and he had won the elections with a landslide in his chiefdom. Would he be wrong or right to be on his side? The crowd was astonished as they watched their chief and member of parliament walk out on them. It took them quite some time to recover from the shock and all they could do was disperse to their different homes looking like people who were returning from a graveyard.

After they had gone a short distance from the gathering, the politician asked the chief?

"Don't you think these people deserve a decent answer on this issue of a town hall?"

"Decent answer? Whoever told you, subjects deserve decency from their rulers? What kind of politician are you? Don't you see they're all hungry? Stuff their hands with a few francs and all those mouths will shut up."

"Aren't you sure, your royal highness, that this blatant betrayal would only make them continue to grieve?"

"Let them continue to grieve, it's good for them. Aren't they a part of the constituency you represent? Griefland constituency? Don't worry, I have their medicine, which is quite simple: a cow or two, and a few bags of rice, and the grieving will turn into grinning.

"I think you're right, your royal highness. His royal highness is always right," said the politician, with a grin.

When the politician was on his own, in the safety of his home, he reflected deeply on the events of the day. He wondered whether he should continue to rely on chief Nyukechen who believed so much in politics of the stomach.

4

With the so much talk about alleviating poverty, he wondered whether there was any future in such politics. Besides, of what use is being a representative of a people only because you want to dupe them. If he had to count on his conscience then he would submit his resignation as MP but because the title was very important for him, he decided not to listen to the dictates of his conscience. He concluded that in order to remain the politician that he was, he had better be a disciple of his Royal Highness Seseku Chief Nyukechen.

The Sacrificed Lunch Pack

My little girl Alice, curious little creature, looked at me sternly as I walked in. As soon as I slumped on the sofa, she came up to me and asked why I had stayed so long at work. I had to explain painstakingly, to satisfy her. Kids nowadays enjoy having their dads around them, unlike the days I was growing up, when fathers were usually the cats of the home and the children the mice. Their absence was usually a great joy for the children. It was usually the time they had freedom of speech, laughter and self expression.

After I had explained my lateness that evening, I asked my little girl Alice if there was anything else she wanted to know. She said there wasn't for the time being, but that she had a suggestion to make to me.

"What is it Alice?" I asked.

"It is like this, daddy, I no longer want to be carrying a lunch pack to school."

"You mean, lunch is no longer necessary for you?"

"No, daddy, I want lunch but I no longer want to take a lunch pack to school."

"I don't understand Alice, you want lunch and you don't want to take a lunch pack to school. You want your lunch to be wrapped up in leaves or paper or what exactly", I said confused.

"Once again, it is like this daddy, I would like you and mummy to replace the lunch pack with a five hundred francs piece each time I'm going to school. I'll use the money to buy lunch at school."

"Now Alice, that surprises me a lot because your mother and I think that your lunch pack is fresher, nicer and surer. That's why you should have it instead of a five hundred francs piece."

"Daddy I know all that but this is what I want. I'm one of the few pupils in my class who come every day to school with a lunch pack in their bag."

"Ah well, you think at thirteen you're too old to go around with a lunch pack. I do take a lunch pack to my office, you know."

"Daddy, so you see, it is not a matter of age or looking down on the idea of a lunch pack. It is simply that I no longer want to take it to school."

"All right my little girl, I'll look into the matter and then discuss it with your mother.

The following week, instead of the splendid lunch pack my little girl Alice used to carry in her school bag, she began going to school every morning with a five hundred francs piece in the left pocket of her skirt. Her mummy had put up a very strong argument in her daughter's favour. She thought that Alice wanted to start managing her own finances and so she should be given the opportunity. My arguments against the unhealthy conditions of the food that was sold in the premises of the school and outside, did not quite make much sense to my wife, so I gave in, hoping my little girl Alice was going to reverse the situation shortly after. But the days went by and then weeks too and my little girl Alice seemed to be getting happier and happier with the new situation. At the end of the term she came back home with wonderfully improved results.

"Come on my little girl, what's the secret," I asked.

"Well daddy, the secret is obvious. The five hundred francs piece that had replaced the lunch pack had done the magic."

"How? Did it make you eat better?"

"No, daddy, it didn't make me eat better. It made me know better."

"Know what dear."

"Know that I could save money and buy marks from my teachers."

"What did you say, dear?"

"Daddy but you heard me."

"No ...eh yes. I might have heard you but I didn't understand. Can you say it again?"

"Ok daddy, I said, I knew that I could save money and buy marks from my teachers."

"Buy what? From whom?"

"Marks daddy, are you deaf?"

"From who?"

"From my teachers. They sell marks. They're not well paid and that's what they do to brave the economic chaos that's been hanging around everywhere in the country."

"You mean, your teachers sell marks?"

"Yes they do daddy. So you didn't know? There are parents who buy marks for their children to enable them have good results," said my little girl Alice.

"So why didn't you tell me?"

"I thought you knew, daddy, but you were just being unkind and unfair to me, so I decided to sacrifice my lunch pack."

"My little girl Alice, if I understand you well, the good result you have produced and which I was so proud of a while ago, result from the obnoxious sale of marks by your teachers to their pupils. And you bought the marks by misleading your parents to succumb to the idea of letting you exercise your rights. My dear little girl, I'm awfully sorry to say this but we have sacrificed you and your entire generation."

There are Orders and
there are Orders

Pius Ake was at his second post, after he had left every young person's dream school, the National School of Administration and Magistracy. He was serving as a Sub divisional Officer . He liked his job very much and whenever anyone cared to listen, he boasted that his was the best job in the entire wide world. When asked why he thought so, he would say that he was the *chef de terre*. A *chef de terre* simply meant the chief landowner. Who on earth can consider him or herself better than a landowner? Moreover, a chief of landowners? The job meant quite a lot to Pius and he enjoyed it very much.

One day, a man, a septuagenarian came to see him.

'Yes what can I do for you sir,' Pius Ake asked.

'Well, *chef de terre*, I'm a retired policeman. I had served our country for forty years and when it was time for me to retire I decided to move to my small house that I had built in a quiet corner in the city. All was all right until one businessman decided to establish a drinking place next door to my house. If his customers only drank and went away quietly I would not have minded, but their drinking is accompanied by loud noise, music and wild dancing. This goes on until the small hours of the morning. In this kind of situation my family and I can hardly catch some sleep. This is my problem, *chef de terre*. Only you can handle it and I believe you'd find a solution to it. Help me *chef*." he said pleadingly.

Pius Ake listened to the old man attentively and then assured him that he was going to look into the complaint and try to find a solution.

"Thank you my son. Thank you. God bless you," the old man said and left.

The following day Pius went to the location himself and found the drinking place. Later in the evening he went there and got a seat and a drink. He sat there from eight o'clock to nine o'clock and there was no sign of the bar closing for the day. He walked up to the young man behind the counter and asked,

"Isn't it time to close yet?"

"Close? This early?" he replied, casually.

"When do you usually close?"

"1.00 a.m, 2.00 a.m. It depends"

"It depends on what?"

"On the customers of course. When the last customer leaves, we too lock up."

"I see. It doesn't depend on the law," Pius Ake murmured to himself.

While he was talking to the man behind the counter, he noticed the operating license of the bar. It was an off license bar which should operate without sitting places and should close by eight o'clock in the evening. The next day, he called the gendarmes in the locality to verify the activities of the bar. They did and gave him feedback. He had been operating the place as an on license bar whereas he had not been licensed to do so. Mr. Ake wrote a service note to the proprietor of the bar, warning him, especially, about the non-respect of the closing hours. Four days later, the proprietor had not bothered to react, so Mr. Ake requested the gendarmes to seal up the bar. He duly informed his immediate boss about it.

The septuagenarian was very pleased about the action and he went back to thank Pius Ake for a service well executed.

It was not quite two weeks when the bar re-opened and the situation was the same. Mr. Ake found this rather worrisome as he had not ordered for the reopening. As he thought about this the old man came in to report that the proprietor had come to confront him and had said that

"There were orders and there were orders."After saying this he left and the following day the bar was opened again. I thought that he had come to bribe you to reverse your order but later I heard that it was your boss who had done it. "Leave it to me," the man said, "your boss is my brother from the same village, I shall handle the matter myself."

"Handle it how" Pius wondered. However, he went to discuss the matter with his boss and all he told him was, "just leave the matter as it is."

"I wonder how I can just leave it like that, when my orders have been flaunted so flagrantly,"

"Well, young man, don't get so heated up. There are orders and there are orders. I hope you understand me."

"Yes I do sir," Pius Ake said and left.

Two weeks later, the bar was again sealed up. This time by a 'prefectoral' order. Shortly after, Mr. Ake met the septuagenarian.

"How did you do it?" he asked.

"I told you I was going to handle the matter. So I did."

"But how," Mr. Ake insisted.

"Well I went to your boss's office crying like a woman whose beloved partner had just died. Tears running down my cheeks frighteningly, which shocked him a lot. In my tradition, if a man of my age sheds tears, then it must be a very serious matter. So when I explained to him what my problem was, he acted with so much celerity."

"So your tears did the trick?"

"If you say so."

Meanwhile, the bar proprietor had not gone to sleep. He moved on to even higher quarters – the Governor. He told the Governor his story and Mr. Governor believed every centimetre of it and promised to wrest him out of the claws of vicious vultures, who instead of serving the people because of whom they had been employed, would want to, like vampires, suck them dry of the blood that keeps them alive. He acted very swiftly. The bar was reopened with immediate effect and before Pius Ake and his boss could digest what was going on, each of them heard their transfer being read on the airwaves of the national radio, one to the Far West and the other to the Far East.

Another Murder in the Cathedral

When Father Kikisangi joined the priesthood, he thought that he had got himself out of the bickering that goes on in the larger society. Far from it, the priesthood is made of ordinary people, not saints. And so he has realized that there is no escape from bickering. At his first post, there was a Father Blondo about whom the whole parish bickered. And a lot of what they talked about was half true and sometimes completely true. For example, whenever he was approached for a funeral mass or to go and pray for someone who was very ill, he would stretch his hand and open his palm in front of the requesting person and say 'money for hand, back for ground'. And as soon as the money gets into his hand, the rest will work out like magic. Father Blondo was also well known for taking advantage of vulnerable women who came for confession or for counselling. As a result, some of the women competed in the shirt market as to who should offer the best shirt to the man of God.

One day, Father Blondo invited Father Kikisangi to a nightclub. The latter was very surprised at the invitation but on second thoughts he said to himself, 'seeing is believing' and accepted to go with him and see. So the two men of God went to have a good time in *Sugar Baby*, a very popular nightclub in the city. Father Blondo was dressed in blue jeans and a tee shirt with the inscription *watch out I'm crazily sexy*, boldly written on it. Father Kikisangi who was dressed in a green pin-striped shirt over a grey pair of trousers, found Father Blondo's dressing inappropriate and

15

he told him so. But Father Blondo asked him what he thought could be more appropriate for a nightclub. A question he could not readily give an answer to. In the nightclub, while Kikisangi was drinking orange juice, Blondo was drinking whisky and beer. Soon after, he got to the dancing floor while Kikisangi sat and watched. His dancing soon simmered like a cooking pot on fire, and then went into a frenzy. Suddenly, he found himself inside a ring which had been spontaneously formed by other very excited dancers. He was in the ring with a tall slim girl in her late teens who was dressed in a skirt that stood many centimetres above her knees, and her top was a sleeveless blouse that projected the generosity of her breasts. She wriggled her waists with the flexibility of a snake and this lit the fire in the man of God, who almost displaced a hip bone in an attempt to outdo the young lady. Father Kikisangi thought it was becoming crazy - a priest in a dancing ring with a near-naked girl. He got up and went into the ring and rescued Blondo from it. He took him out of the nightclub and put him in the back seat of the car. He immediately slumped and only minutes afterwards he was snoring. Father Kikisangi drove back to the parish and managed to get Father Blondo to his room. He laid him in bed and then went to bed himself. While in bed, Father Kikisangi wondered whether he had done the right thing to have gone to *Sugar Baby*.

"It might not have been the right thing," thought he "but I got a fellow priest out of an awkward situation and I also learnt a lot from the experience. People need to wrestle and wriggle out the tension in them and they can do it through music and dance. I saw the rationale for the rollicking situation in many churches these days, where hard rock music has replaced solemn songs of praise to the Heavenly Father. I also realized that the churches have so much to do to give humanity the elixir it needs to cope with the twists and turns of modern living."

16

Father Kikisangi slept off as thought after thought tortured his mind.

At breakfast he asked Father Blondo how he felt that morning.

"Good, very good," replied Father Blondo.

"I'm glad you're fine. I hope you remember you were drunk last night."

"Me, drunk. How dare you say I was drunk. Me drunk, a reverend father drunk. You must be out of your mind."

"Me, out of my mind. I should be if you can't remember that last night, you and I were both in a night club called *Sugar Baby*."

"No, I don't remember. I know sometimes I go to nightclubs but I don't remember having gone to any last night and worse still with you."

"In that case, you're right. I must be out of my mind." Father Kikisangi said derisively.

After this incident Father Kikisangi took time off to question his sanity, and arrived at the conclusion that he could be everything but insane. He wondered how people like Father Blondo fared so well in the church – a very religious setting.

At the end of the year, it was welcome relief for him when he moved to Saint Pius University as a teacher. Saint Pius University was gradually building up a reputation of excellence in a society where excellence had been condemned and thrown to hungry dogs. So, when SPU was being set up it was hoped that it would bring back excellence.

Unfortunately, excellence is very dependent on people. There is usually an effort to identify excellent people to inculcate excellence in especially the young. So SPU did not only consider academic but also moral excellence in the selection of its teachers and other staff. Father Kikisangi felt very elated and assured when he was called upon to teach there. He went there in good faith and worked not only diligently but also honestly and with an open mind. His good reputation could hardly hide from the evaluation of the students he taught. The higher authorities of the institution could not help coming to terms with this positive reputation and Father Kikisangi was rewarded with a high position. He had not yet had a professorial chair but he was elected to the exalted position of Deputy Vice Chancellor. He saw this as an opportunity to serve the church and the nation he loved so much. He took up the office and performed so well that he was likely to be one of the candidates to be short listed for the replacement of Father Candid Yamben, the Vice Chancellor, whose tenure of office expires at the end of the academic year. Unfortunately, this did not go down well with his boss the Vice Chancellor. As Deputy Vice Chancellor, his boss had tried to associate him with deals that were to make them both make some extra money but he had on each occasion turned down his proposal. This, the boss did not like and so Father Kikisangi was invariably, not liked. Father Candid candidly did everything to bring his deputy to disrepute. He accused him of preaching violence in his sermons, which did not augur well for a country that prided itself on peace. Also, he usually missed out on his prayer sessions and finally he was a drunkard. Father Kikisangi's reputation continued to soar, in spite of, Father Candid's desperate efforts to candidly bring it down.

The news spread on the campus like wildfire. Father Kikisangi is the Vice Chancellor-elect. Everybody of the Saint Pius University community was happy except the incumbent Vice Chancellor and his cohorts. The news had almost swept him off his feet. When he found himself still standing upright, he swore that Kikisangi would only succeed him over his dead body. He therefore started a ploy to destroy him. He immediately swung into action by inviting one of his cohorts, a teacher in the university called, Reverend Sister Rosa, to his office.

"Sister, thanks for reacting promptly to my invitation," said Father Candid.

"You're welcome Father. I always take everything from you candidly," replied Sister Rosa.

"Now Rosa, first of all turn the door knob. I wouldn't want any interruptions."

"Done boss."

"Let's get down to business then. Have you heard the news?"

"What news Father?"

"The news that has spread here on campus like wildfire."

"You mean the news about Father Kikisangi? That he is your likely replacement?"

"Exactly. Can you imagine Kikisangi becoming my successor, the boss of this institution?"

"No boss. I've never liked that man. He pretends to be the purest priest the church has ever had. If he becomes the Vice Chancellor, I'd resign from this University."

"God forbid. He can't become the boss here. He's a dangerous man."

"But he's been elected already. We're only waiting for confirmation from the higher quarters."

"I bet, he won't have the confirmation. Not while I'm still breathing this pure air."

"So what are you up to Father?"

"Wake up sister, wake up! We're going to smear him with despicable acts of fornication. It will be like smearing someone with shit to wade off any imaginable acquaintance. First of all you're going to arrange with two attractive looking female students. They have confessed to you that the upright father, Kikisangi has made love to them and then you've carried out investigations and found that the allegation is true. Finally you'll take the matter to the higher quarters. They will appreciate it better than you and me and take the appropriate action."

"What if the girls refuse to cooperate, Father?"

"Then you make them cooperate."

"Make, how?"

"Wake up, wake up Sister. You know what to do. I know, you know."

Sister Rosa left the office and one week later she went knocking at the door of the pro chancellor of SPU.

"Your Lordship, I'm so sorry to come and disturb you at this time but it is rather urgent."

"Yes, Sister Rosa, what's it?"

"You see these girls standing here have a very strange story to tell."

"Strange story to tell. By the way, who are they?"

"This is Ngo Biaba, and this Ngo Babs. Both of them students of the faculty of philosophy at the University."

"Yes my girls, what's your story?"

"Well, your Lordship, it is like this, Father Kikisangi has almost turned me into a housewife," said Ngo Biaba.

"My daughter, what do you mean? Have you been cooking for him?

"No your Lordship. He's been having me sleep with him almost every night."

"So, why are you telling me this only now."

"I want the relationship to stop."

"Why do you want it to stop."

"Because I've had what I wanted from him."

"What did you want from him?"

"Favours in the courses he was teaching. I'm done with them."

"Do you realize these are very serious allegations you are making against a priest — a man of God?"

"I do your Lordship?"

"And you Ngo … what again?"

"Ngo Babs, your Lordship."

"Yes Ngo Babs, what do you have to say?"

20

"Your Lordship, for some time now, Father Kikisangi has been making passes at me. He fondles my backside each time he meets me. In fact, he wants to have sex with me at all cost. He appears to me even in my dreams."

"That's all right. I've heard enough. Thank you very much."

After the trio had left, his Lordship felt completely consumed with anger, especially because the allegations had to do with Father Kikisangi, a man in whom he had invested so much trust. He was so angry that he lost the common sense of inviting Father Kikisangi to hear his own side of the story.

Shortly after, news about the meeting with his Lordship had spread on the campus. The news got from ear to ear but it took quite some time for it to get to Father Kikisangi himself. He was chatting very excitingly with Sister Rosa and one student who had heard the story was very surprised. He waited until the end of the chat and then cornered Father Kikisangi to find out what was going on. He realized that the reverend gentleman had no inkling of what was all over the place. It was then the student told him about what the trio had done.

Father Kikisangi felt very embarrassed and was shocked. When he recovered from the shock, he drove straight to the residence of his Lordship.

As soon as his Lordship saw him he started bullying and shouting, "You traitor, you let me down, you let me down, how could you of all people do this to me. You know how much esteem I have had for you and then you let me down like this. Getting involved in fornication with your own students and taking advantage of the vulnerability of young people you are supposed to mould. You're a big disappointment and I tell you I'll throw up if I continue to see you standing there."

"Your Lordship, I'm very disappointed that you'd get information like this and you'd not give me the chance to defend myself before taking sides."

"You didn't need any defence. The matter had been carefully investigated by Reverend Sister Rosa before it was brought to me. Once again Father Kikisangi, you're an embarrassment to me and of course the church. The earlier you leave this place the faster you'd safe me the trouble of throwing up.

Father Kikisangi left the residence and drove to the cathedral. As usual, the doors were wide open and he put his palms together in humility and total submission to God Almighty. He walked gently towards the altar. On the first step of the altar, he knelt down and muttered: This is a murder, yet another murder, in the cathedral.

He took another step upwards and knelt down in prayer:

Our father in heaven
Only you can have the patience
To listen to me, for I have excrement all over me.
I thank You, I still have the strength and courage
To come to your presence
Knowing it's you and only you
Can see through the minds of people.
I kneel not to ask for my own forgiveness
But for that of those who persecute me.
Let your light shine O Lord, on Saint Pius University
And the same for our beloved country.

Father Kikisangi rose from the altar , his palms still clasped together prayerfully, and walked to the outlet of the cathedral. When he stepped out, he un-clasped his hands and walked gently to his car. While he was driving through the darkness, his headlights shone on the faces of some of the people in the street, walking along as if they admired darkness and then she slowed down at spot where there were deep potholes. Suddenly, three teenage girls rushed to his car as if they wanted to request for a ride. He stopped and all three of them asked: "do you need any service?"

"Service. What service?"Father Kiki asked.

"The type of service we offer. You know, we make men like you feel good. Feel really good. Just try me," they said at the same time.

Father Kikisangi was very embarrassed. He looked at himself and noticed that he was not wearing his cassock. So he simply pressed on his accelerator and drove on into the darkness.

By the time he got to his residence, he understood one other thing: the reason for the so much madness going on in our cities.

My Command at a Lamidat

I had just taken command as a Senior Divisional
Officer in a Lamidat. There was obviously a reigning
Lamido, the traditional ruler of the people. Shortly
before my installation I had gone to him to pay homage. He
commanded so much respect, especially from his people.
They never looked at him directly when they spoke to him.
Even before speaking to him they had to bow down. The
women covered their mouths as they spoke to him. He was
a little above six feet and he made himself taller by raising
his shoulders whenever he was standing up. The airs around
him would make every bystander think that he deserved
his job.

On the day I was being installed, he and his entourage
actually stole the show. In defiance of protocol he arrived
last at the ceremonial grounds. He was sitting majestically
on a white horse that was flanked at each side by two brown
horses. As soon as his horse touched the ceremonial ground,
there was a loud trumpet blast. Spontaneously everyone
stood up and all was at a standstill. About twenty horses
rode majestically past the grandstand and at the end the
Lamido's horses came through and halted at the grandstand.
Four hefty men went to the horse and carried the Lamido,
each man holding an edge of the rods that held the
hammock. Carefully, he was placed in his chair that had the
skin of a tiger spread on it. As soon as he had settled, the
trumpeting stopped, the horsemen dispersed and took their
places behind the grandstand. The dignitaries in the
grandstand, who had been spellbound on the arrival of the
Lamido sat down and the ceremony continued from where

25

it had been interrupted. A few minutes later, it was all over and those who had been given special invitation cards were to go over to the residence of the S.D.O for a grand reception. Before the protocol officials could start ushering dignitaries out, the Lamido's trumpeters again blasted their trumpets and took everyone by surprise. Suddenly, a glittering car glided towards the grandstand. It was limousine, a Silver Bird. It was the first time the Lamido was making the car public. The entire crowd was seeing it for the first time. So, they looked at it very curiously. The Lamido was escorted from his seat and led to the car. When he got in and sat down, there was uproar, people cheering, drumming and dancing. He waved to them as he drove off silently and they shouted and glorified him. He had defied protocol and stolen the show. I felt belittled but I tried very hard not to show it.

I knew from then that my greatest stumbling block in the locality was the Lamido himself. So I planned to make him understand that I was not only the administrative head of the whole division but also the personal representative of the President of the Republic. He seemed to have preempted my plans and summoned me to his palace the very next day. When he met me he said:

"Mr. S.D.O. I didn't understand why the national anthem was not sung on my arrival at the ceremonial ground?"

The question came very unexpectedly and I had to think before giving an answer. It took me a good sixty-five seconds before I could find appropriate words for His Royal Highness the Lamido. He even had to remind me to give him an answer.

"Your Royal Highness, you remember you came late to the ceremony. Before you came the anthem had been sung."

"What did you say? The Lamido was late? Me, late for an occasion in my Lamidat. I've never been told anything like that. I hope you know your responsibilities very well and limits of such responsibilities. Now let me tell you, as the head of this Lamidat, I arrive last, and leave first for every official ceremony in this Lamidat. If you didn't know that then you have a lot to learn about this locality."

I left the Lamidat feeling very disappointed and confused, wondering whether our country had different laws from locality to locality.

Two weeks later, I heard a knock on my door at an unholy time of 1.30 a.m. I wondered what the matter was. If it was that urgent, whoever it was should have telephoned. And besides, the guards let him come into the premises, without asking his consent. I got out of bed and enquired who it was.

"Messengers from the Lamido," the guard said.

"What do they want at this time? Why couldn't they wait to come later in the morning?"

"They said their business was very urgent and besides, they are messengers from the Lamido."

"O.K let them in," I said, sitting in one of the armchairs.

Five hefty men came in , looking like people who enjoyed putting up with trouble. I asked them what business they were up to.

"The Lamido has sent us with a message," said one of them.

"Where's it?"

"Outside."

"Outside! You come in leaving the message outside?"

"So, how do I get it?"

"By moving to it. You have to come along with us."

"Come along with you! You know who you're dealing with, don't you?"

"Of course we do. The Senior Divisional Officer, isn't it?" they asked confidently.

It was getting rather scary but I made up my mind to follow them. Outside my premises a ten-ton lorry had been parked with the driver still behind the steering wheel. In it were bags of rice, wheat and barely. There were also two live cows that had been well tied up in the lorry. As if that was not enough, there were cartons of vegetable oil and even wine.

"All these for me?" I asked.

"All these for you," the spokesman answered.

My mind went riot as to what to do. "Why should the Lamido be so generous to me? What was behind it? What should I do?"

At this point, the spokesman said that all the goods in the lorry were gifts from the Lamido to the Senior Divisional Officer. It was traditional for the Lamido to offer every Government Official who had been posted to his Lamidat some gifts, and this was done discreetly. This explained why the presentation was being carried out at that time of the day. Before he could say anything, the spokesperson had asked that the truck be offloaded. Within thirty minutes, the lorry was emptied and the five men jumped in and drove away, deep into the silence of the night. I still did not understand what all that meant but I decided to go back to bed and tried to sleep.

Before going to work that morning, I called my wife and showed her the presents from the Lamidat.

"Darling this is wonderful, all these for us. The Lamido must be a darling," she said very excited. "Nowhere have we ever been honored with so many gifts. I had earlier resented coming here in the north but now I think whoever thought of sending us here on transfer had done a very good thing, for us. With two cows, I'm not sure we shall buy meat for the next six months, and all these food items. We've really been spoiled by the Lamido. I'm really dying to meet him."

"Don't get too excited woman. Lamidos have little respect for women. So you should be careful, if you're already making any plans to meet him. The way I look at all these gifts is different. The Lamido obviously needs the support of the administration to sustain the high-handed authority he has over his people and so one of his tactics is to bribe the Senior Divisional Officer, who happens to be me."

"And who are you to refuse such generous bribe? Bribe coming from a whole Lamido. I bet, you deny, you die," my wife said persuasively.

"It would not be me to want you dead. Not at this age and at a time when the children are still young. The things have already been accepted, anyway," she said conclusively.

I looked at my wife doubtfully and then went to the car that was waiting to take me to my office. I sat in the back seat, not knowing how I felt. The driver ignited and we were office bound.

The Barren Womb

It's insane to think that children are incidental in marriage', Kula thought as he kept wriggling his wrist. He had just been told how worthless he was in keeping a wife who had been unable to bare him children and how foolish he was, not to have gone out and fetch children. He had been married to his beautiful wife ten years earlier but they had not been blessed with a child. During and soon after their honey moon, the idea of children was taken for granted. It was but normal that children be born after a marriage, and they were going to come when the time was right. But years had come and gone and they had become tired of waiting, and eventually tired of each other. When it finally dawned on them that the exuberant noise of a child or children in their home, could be a catalyst to their ebbing love, the couple became desperate. After aborted trials with different gynecologists, they decided to meet a traditional healer, commonly called native doctor.

Mami Dudu had been childless until the over ripe age of forty-two. She had given up ever having a child but something happened to assuage her pessimism. A childhood friend of hers had settled in the heart of the equatorial rain forest and the people there were experts in plant medication. They knew which tree bark treats what disease. Human fertility was not a problem among these people. All a woman needed do was accept enema and the bark of one of the trees was boiled overnight and she took the stuff once every other day, seven times. So when Nani ran into Mami Dudu, she was scandalized to find out that her friend was childless.

She instantly arranged that Mami Dudu must go back to the equatorial forest with her. She did and had the treatment. When she returned to her husband, it did not take them two months to notice that she was heavy with child. After two other births, Mama Dudu decided to go back to the heart of the forest and train as a native doctor. She devoted the rest of her life making women with fertility problems give birth. When Kula heard about her, he could not wait to take his wife there. Nirina, Kula's wife stayed at Mami Dudu's for two months, religiously undergoing the treatment. When she returned to her husband she was sure things would happen. But several months went by and nothing happened. At this point Kula decided to meet a soothsayer.

'Pa Nkankan, tell me what's going on. I'm young and strong and as soon as I knew I could take care of a wife, I decided to get married. I loved my wife and she loved me too and we thought we should crown the love with an issue. But I'm afraid I've waited long enough for that issue. That's why I ask the question, what's going on?'

The soothsayer looked at him steadily for a full minute. Then he shook his head in disappointment, without saying anything.

'Pa say something', Kula said pleadingly. 'I would like to hear you say something.'

Pa Nkankan just looked on in silence. Then he moved towards a curtain in the middle of the room. He pulled it gently and it opened into his temple. He took out his prediction paraphernalia, recited some incantations and peered into a calabash. When he took up his head, he shook it as if to confirm his fears.

'Your wife has a barren womb', he announced.

'Barren womb? What does that mean?' Kula asked desperately.

'If you must hear from my mouth, she cannot have children. Her womb is as barren as a desert,' Pa said bluntly.

'So, what do I do?' asked Kula.

'Do like everyone does. Take another wife.'

Kula was confused. He had taken time to cultivate love, like a devoted gardener would do a flower garden. It has been costly in time, money and will, and then he was being advised to take another wife. Take another wife because he must have children.

'It wasn't worth it. No, it wasn't worth taking another wife', he said leaving the soothsayer's house.

'My bill!' shouted the soothsayer.

'Oh your bill! You'll have it next time,' he shouted back distastefully.

'I see why astute business people insist on payment before service,' the soothsayer said grudgingly.

Back home, Kula became restless. There was nothing around him that could please him. Not even Nirina, his wife. He decided he would contact Kapgun, his childhood friend. Unfortunately, it was a weekend and the man had gone to his village. He had to wait for Monday. At exactly eight o'clock that Monday, Kula left for Kapgun's office. He was afraid he might not be in the office. Absence on Monday mornings was not unusual. Public workers usually complained of weekend hangover. So, as soon as he got a response after his knock, he was much relieved.

"Hello kula kula, long time, no see. It must be something that doesn't belong to our world that brings you here at this time of day. Or are my eyes playing tricks on me?"Kapgun asked looking very surprised.

"No, your eyes can't be playing tricks on you at this age. They still have a long way to serve you with utmost diligence. It's me Kula in flesh and spirit. I have come to see you because I had contacted a soothsayer who has informed me that my wife is barren and if I was interested in having children I should look for another woman and marry."

"In that case, sit down and let's talk," Kapgun said.

Kula pulled out the visitor's chair and sat down. Kapgun wondered why it had been so difficult for his friend to have any children. He examined his own situation, where the children were coming at an alarming rate. Sometimes they even come in pairs. He said he was already burdened with eight children to bring up. He was looking for a way of stopping them from coming. Kula told him, he had been patient all along, believing that children were one of those mysterious gifts from the almighty God. He was waiting for that day that He the Almighty will intervene.

"But when the soothsayer starts saying things like a barren womb, I get very disturbed," Kula said with much disappointment.

"In this case, go back to the village and find out what the soothsayer actually means or whether there's substance in what he has said," Kapgun advised.

Kula took his friend's advice and decided to go to his village, which was only thirty kilometres from the town, to complain to the oldest man who invariably was the wisest. The man had been his father's best friend when he was alive. A week after he had taken the decision Kula took a bush taxi, usually called *opep* and headed towards his village. After two hours of a very rough drive, he arrived in his village. He was covered with mud as he and the other passengers had spent much energy and time to pull out the vehicle each time it got stuck in mud. He needed to clean himself up, so he went first to their family compound. He asked for water which was brought to him in an eight-litre bucket. He took it to the back of one of the houses and had a refreshing bath. He then dressed up, ate some food and went to T'akali's home. So, the old one was called. He was a notable in the village and so he owned a compound with three buildings making up a u-shape if one stood backing the central building, which was also the main building where the old man himself lived. The other two buildings which stood face-to-face, were occupied by his wives and their children. In addition to his much wisdom, T'akali was a very good manager. He was able to manage his household, which consisted six wives and thirty-six children, without any problems. His six wives loved one another so much that the community branded them as women from one womb. To many, T'akali was simply lucky in his choice of wives. Because of the love that reigned among the women, peace was very obvious. The children were bathed in peace and harmony and so they grew up becoming very successful. Among his thirty-six children, there were already two medical doctors, four lawyers, two accountants, five teachers, four engineers and three farmers. In front of the main building was a mango tree that also served as a shade. T'akali was sitting under the tree with a long broom in his right hand. He used it to drive off houseflies. When he took up his head and his eyes caught mine, I immediately greeted:

"Good afternoon old one."

"Good afternoon my son. What's it you want from me. You hardly ever come here on a week day, like this."

"I've come to you because something very strange has happened to me and I believe it's your wisdom that will put my spirits back on course."

"Sit down first of all my son. Do you need some fresh water to drink?"

"Yes, that's very thoughtful."

Kula drank two cups of water, took a deep breath and felt much relaxed.

"Now, can you tell me what this strange thing that has happened to you is?"

"Yes of course, old and wise one, I've spent all that I have in terms of money, material and time on a woman, who of course is my wife but so far I haven't harvested a single fruit from the marriage."

"What do you mean, you haven't harvested a single fruit," T'akali asked?

"I mean no child. Not even a pregnancy," answered Kula. "A few days ago someone even told me she has a barren womb."

"That's quite strange. In my eighty years of existence no such thing has happened to anyone I know," T'akali said shaking his head sadly. "The great God can't create a woman with a barren womb."

"No old one, but that's how sad my situation is," Kula insisted.

"Have you found out everything about the woman's family?" T'akali asked.

"Yes old one."

"No curse?"

"No curse, old one."

"Did you give food to your ancestors before starting your marriage negotiations?"

"Yes I did."

"Before you took your wife to the matrimonial bed, was she cleansed?"

"Yes, she was."

"Now, what about the money to marry her? I mean money for the bride price. How did you get it?"

"How I got the money? That was a long time ago"

"Yes, it was a long time ago but you should still remember how you got it. What was the source of the money."

"Source of money?"

"Yes, source of money. How did it come about? Did it germinate like a plant or was it a bank loan?"

"No, not at all. It wasn't a loan. It was some sort of manna, Yes manna from heaven."

"Manna from heaven! That must be very interesting. Tell me more about this manna eh…eh money from heaven," the old man said looking very interested.

"Well," said Kula "it sometimes happens, you know. For example there was this couple, somewhere in one of the countries of the white man, who got up one morning and found their courtyard green with banknotes. Husband and wife spent the whole morning putting the notes together in bags. When they had finished they sat together to consider the next line of action. First, they established that they were genuine notes and then invited the police and the press to tell them their story. It was concluded that a suitcase of money might have fallen off a flying aircraft, bursting open and spilling out its content in the courtyard. Adverts were therefore put in different newspapers, requesting anyone who might have lost money to come up and claim it, but nobody did. After one, two and even three months, the police officially declared the couple, the sole proprietors of the money. Wouldn't you call that manna from heaven?" asked Kula.

"Indeed it was manna from heaven and your story has just reminded me of another story I know very well. In those days, when one of my sons was working in the capital city and I was staying with him, following up my pension file, he returned home one day looking very worried. When I asked him what the matter was, he said that something strange had happened to his boss. There had been a fault in the electrical installation in his official residence and he had given instructions that it should be verified and repaired. So an electrician was invited to do the job. He had to go into the ceiling where he did not only identify the electrical fault but also discovered something unusual. Five-figure banknotes had been neatly packed in cartons at one corner of the ceiling. He carefully climbed down, went to a nearby store and bought a large plastic bag and climbed back into the ceiling with it and filled it neatly. He corrected the electrical fault and slipped out of the house without any one taking much notice of him. When the boss returned in the evening, he was only too happy that the fault had been corrected. It was only on the seventh day that he discovered what had befallen him.

On that Sunday morning, while his wife and children had gone to church to worship their God, my son's boss had remained at home to worship his – almighty money. As soon as he was all by himself, he got a ladder and climbed into the ceiling. When he set his eyes on the spot where he had kept his god, he knew something had gone wrong. Several times, he hit the torch, he had brought with him. The more he did so, the more nervous he became, hoping it would lit the place better but the situation did not change. Humbly he went on his knees, spread out his arms feeling every corner but he felt no banknote. He sniffed and sniffed every corner but he smelt nothing like a banknote. His breathing was almost stopping when something told him to be a man. Gently, he found his way out of the ceiling. He went to his private living room and slumped in a couch brooding over his money.

"My money, ah my money," he thought. "Hundreds of millions in maximum notes, all gone. Seems like a dream. A very bad dream"

He did not have time enough to weep over his lost wealth because his wife and children had just returned from church. They found him in an unusual way.

"What's wrong with you honey?" asked his wife.

There was an uneasy silence as the man simply looked at his wife wondering how she knew? Then he gathered courage to ask in turn? "Money? What about money?"

"Whose has talked about money? I've simply asked what's wrong with you, honey."

"Ah, honey, I didn't hear you well. Well, it's the gastric pain. It has started again."

"Not again!" she exclaimed. "Should I call Dr Laila?"

"No, don't bother, I hope the pains will go, even if not

as swiftly as they had come. What I need now is to be alone and have some sleep."

He got out of the couch and sluggishly walked to his bed room. He lay down for a long, long time.

"Well," said Kula, "that was the electrician's own manna from heaven."

"Do you think? It could have been manna from hell. The source of the money was unknown," said the old one.

"What do you mean unknown? Was it not from the ceiling of your son's boss?"

"Yes, it was. But tell me, is the inside of a ceiling, the place for hundreds of millions of banknotes?"

"I see your point, old one."

"I'm glad you understand. One has to be careful about such money because genuine happiness can be achieved only when one earns what they have. Remember you still haven't told me about your own manna from heaven."

"You know, old one," Kula began, "my late father loved me so much and he believed a lot in educating his children. He had always told us that earthly salvation was in education. So he sacrificed a lot to send me to Australia for further education. After my postgraduate degree in economics, I decided to return home and be useful to my country. But then, things did not work out as I had thought. After my return, I sojourned in the unemployment train for two years. I was almost getting mentally disturbed when a providential act of the President got me out of the train. I then stumbled on the trail of a career in the Ministry of the Interior.

"While in the capital city, compiling the necessary documents for posting, I ran into a friend who was carrying out the same exercise. He had returned from the Soviet Union a year earlier. As soon as we had finished exchanging greetings, he said:

"Tell you what? It's raining money somewhere in the city."

"How's that?" I asked

"I've just pocketed a whooping one million five hundred thousand francs and it is like this. I was going to deposit my recruitment documents when someone cornered me and asked if I had studied abroad and I said yes. He then asked me to prove it. I became suspicious and asked what he was up to. He took me aside and said that there was this lady who was the owner of a transit company and she had won the contract to transport the luggage of all those who were abroad and had been recruited through the providential act of the President. I told him I did not qualify because I had already returned home and I had been recruited while already in the country. He said it did not matter where I had been recruited. What mattered was simply proof that I had studied abroad. A simple attestation from the University where I had studied was enough. I looked at him and asked if he was sure. He assured me and I simply gave him a photocopy of my result attestation from Patrice Lumumba Friendship University, Moscow and then I indicated my name on the recruitment list. He gave me an address and asked me to meet him the following day. When I got there that day, behold I was given some documents to sign and ten minutes later I was smiling home with the sum I had told you about in my pocket."

"So old one," said Kula, "when my friend told me that story, it sounded almost like a fairy tale but he took out ten thousand francs from his pocket and gave me to help myself. He also gave me the name and address of the man who had informed him about the transaction. The following day, I rushed there and submitted my certificate from Melbourne and indicated my name on the recruitment list. My appointment was much longer. I was asked to come after two weeks. I wondered why it had to be two weeks in my own case. But it gave me time to consider the rationale behind the whole transaction. In my own case I had been through with Melbourne, two years before, and since then I had been looking for a job. Then the providential act came and my name figured on the list, and there was someone going to claim that she had transported my luggage from Australia. She was going to be paid. I didn't-know-how-much but the hope was that I was going to get something out of it. No doubt, my friend had said it was raining money. The two weeks came by and I went to the transit company, signed some papers and I was given the same sum of money as my friend from Moscow. I thought I was going to have more considering the distance between the country and Melbourne. However, in things like that logic was illogical. I pocketed the money and went home. The idea that I did not actually deserve the money worried me for some time but I soon went over it especially because there had been many other beneficiaries like me. There was even the case of someone who had earlier had a job in the administration in a different capacity and had been earning a salary. Then his name came up in the list of beneficiaries of the providential act. He had studied in a neighbouring country and had returned home three years earlier. He too qualified for the luggage transit transaction and he pocketed his own share. In this regard I felt a bit more at ease with the money and then dubbed it manna from heaven. Before I got posted, I took the money home and told my father about it and that I wanted to invest it in having a wife. That's how he got the family together and they took me along to my would-be wife's village. There the bride price was paid and other traditional rituals were carried out. Well, old one, that was the manner in which I got my manna from heaven and also the way in which I made use of it."

The old and wise one shook his head and asked? "My son, do you know if that transit company is still existing?"

"No idea. I haven't had anything to do with it ever since I got the money."

"I would be surprised if it still exists. Companies that thrive on corruption don't thrive for long. What I can say is that the company had arranged a dirty deal with some top officials, taking advantage of the fact that some of the people who had been recruited through the providential act were still abroad, and they had to be encouraged to return home. So, that manna of yours was easy money but it was also crooked in a way. You did not quite deserve it. My son, crooked money may profit in the short term but never in the long term."

"But old one what would I have done? It was raining money as my friend had said. Would it not have been foolish of me not to have taken advantage of the rain?"

"My son, it is not because everyone is bathing in the rain that you too must have your bath in it. You told the story of a couple who got up and found their courtyard full of money. Did they take advantage of the situation? You yourself said it. They duly informed the police and the press. So my son, there's no doubt that your marriage hasn't yielded any fruits because it was founded on crooked money. In life we have to be careful about the things we do. Something, as sacred as marriage, shouldn't be built on drab concepts like corruption. It should be built on a very solid foundation. Solidity here is the abundance of truth, honesty and purity. You and your wife need purification, a lot of it. After that the rest will follow. All isn't lost yet, my boy," the old and wise one said, a subtle smile flickering across his face.

Doctor Kalawa

Calm, meticulous and suave, Dr Kalawa has just qualified as a surgeon. His thesis on oncology was exemplary and it is till date displayed on the website of the medical school he attended. After a brilliant presentation of his end-of-course thesis, which made headlines the world over, he became a hot cake on the job market. Genuine intellectualism does not seem to care about height, sex, nationality nor race. As scrupulous as he was, Dr Kalawa considered all the options at his disposal, including the fat pay packets offered by the different institutions that needed him. He concluded that money wasn't everything. He resolved to pick up himself and his bags and return home. He felt that he would be more useful back home, especially because there, were very few medical doctors. His dear country was unfortunately one of the countries with a very disappointing doctor: patient ratio.

His homecoming was a big relief to his extended family as it aroused a lot of hope. There was a doctor in the family, and the only at that. All the grannies and grand dads who usually felt a pain run through them like electric current would have someone to listen to them, and assure them. Also the young people in the family who have schooling to do would have someone to turn to each time they ran short of books and school fees. His immediate preoccupation was to get a job and settle down. So he immediately applied for one. A month after, he had his first post. He had been sent to head a district hospital in a place called Karafu. Dr Kalawa found out that the hospital was a new creation and there were no structures in place. Karafu itself was a sub-

43

divisional headquarters but to get there required transportation on foot for fifty kilometres, something the doctor had not done all his life. He took the posting as a challenge and was determined to start work. He went to see things for himself. It was a rude shock for him that everything he had heard was true. There was an identified piece of land for the hospital but there was no building on it. Apart from him, no other person had been posted to the hospital, not even a nurse. He felt that it was a waste to post a surgeon, an oncologist for that matter to a non-existing hospital. He returned to the Department of Health and gave his report. Two months went by without any reaction and Dr Kalawa could not help but start complaining, whenever he could. One day he met an acquaintance, Pascalo Olingo, and they started conversing: "Pascalo, can you imagine that I've been technically unemployed for over two months?"

"How's that?"

"On paper I've been recruited and even appointed to head a district hospital. I went to the hospital and found no hospital."

"So?"

"So I've got no place of work."

"What do you mean, no place of work? You mean, you haven't assumed duty?"

"In a way, I have. When I first got there, the Sub-divisional Officer diligently issued a document that I had duly assumed duty and this had been submitted with other documents to ensure that my salary be paid."

"Lucky you. Got a job where there's no job. If I were you, I'd look for a private clinic and work there and make some extra money for myself, pending when they'll make a hospital available for me. Many a citizen have taken advantage of this kind of situation to get into big time businesses or become academics. They use the waiting time to obtain their PhDs and change their titles and their statuses."

"As for me, I have no knack of renewing my title, nor a knack of making fast money, otherwise, I would have remained abroad. My problem is making myself useful. I think I have a knack of serving my people, my wretched people, as I see them."

"That's why the private clinic is the answer. There you'll meet lots of them – helpless people who have lost faith in public hospitals. You'll be useful to them and in addition make some money for yourself."

"Pascalo, I have a responsibility to the district where I've been posted. I think it is my duty to take health to a people who have not known who a medical doctor is since the beginning of existence. They've been given the opportunity to know, so it should be made use of." I want to go and work there and only there."

"My dear friend, no doubt you've only just come. So it's no wonder you don't understand what's going on in the Department of Health. What counts is money, not health. If health counts they won't send a surgeon to a non-existent hospital. How many of you do we have in this country? Twenty surgeons in a country of twenty million people, and then they pretend that they don't know how useful you can be in the few referral hospitals around the country. You're going to wait for years before that hospital will become functional. Here institutions are created at random, simply to satisfy a promise. And the creation, which is quite easy on paper becomes a problem on the ground. And poor you, Dr Kalawa, you have fallen victim to this common impropriety. Had it been you were one of the smart guys, you would have been posted to an appropriate hospital."

"How's being a smart guy?"

"Being smart is bribing your way to positions. If you were smart enough, you would not just have applied for a job, but also followed up to ensure you have the right treatment."

45

"Me, follow up an application for job, when my credentials are so outstanding, medical institutions are begging for my services?"

"Medical institutions where?"

"Abroad where I trained."

"I thought so. Your value is known abroad where you trained, but here who cares. You must belong to the appropriate clan for your worth to gain currency. Otherwise you've got to bribe your way up or anywhere at all. That's how it works."

"So, what do I do?"

"What you do is to forget about your high sounding credentials and be a smart guy. Bribe your way to a better post."

In spite of Pascalo's advice, Dr Kalawa hoped that things would eventually change. But as time went by, the inelasticity of his hope dropped. Two years had gone by without any change at Karafu. His dream job was in no way, coming his way. However, he had started earning a salary. This made him even more uncomfortable as he felt that he did not deserve it. He had always known that a salary should be earned. He was faced with a perplexing situation, where he was being paid for a job he had duly been employed, but he was doing nothing to earn it. He had to engage in a long discussion with his conscience and the result was that it was not his fault that he was doing nothing. His name was in the paymasters roll and it did not matter to the said paymaster whether he did his job or not. It was the duty of the appropriate authorities to give information about people who did not do their jobs and order that their salaries be suspended. So, as long as the salary continued to be deposited in his account at the end of each month it was his right to sign out the money for use. Besides, that was his only source of income. This situation persisted for another year. Karafu people continued to live on the false hope that their hospital would soon start. Dr Kalawa got very close to falling in the temptation to check out of the country he loved so much and has sacrificed a brilliant medical career for. One day, he ran into Pascalo again.

"Hello docta, how's life?"

"Not inspiring at all. I've been technically knocked out of activity. Three years have folded up and I've not made use of a surgery knife. This is not healthy for me, in all respect,." said Dr Kalawa disappointingly.

"Well, I had earlier told you. Here is a country with a difference. You must bribe to get recognized, no matter how worthy and useful you might be. So, what are you waiting for? I'm afraid you'll wait for a very long time if you insist on only doing the right."

A week later, Dr Kalawa went to the Department of Health to see the Personnel Officer. He booked for audience and was ushered into the office thirty minutes later. It was a cozy office, with perfect air conditioning and expensive furnishing. The Personnel Officer a man in his thirties, sat behind his oversize desk with the caption: *No Stress,* clearly written on his forehead. Kalawa looked at him enviously, talking silently to himself that the young man must be enjoying his job. He was not a medical doctor like himself but he sure enjoyed placing doctors at their different posts.

"Good day, sir." Kalawa said.

"Yes, can I help you?"

"You see, sir, I'm Dr Kalawa."

"Yes, I know." The P.O. said arrogantly.

"In that case you know my problem so well."

"Er..er. your problem. What problem?"

Kalawa was very surprised at the question but he went on to explain.

"My problem is like this. I had been recruited three years ago and posted to head a non-existent hospital. When I discovered, that was the case, I duly complained but I was told that the hospital had been created and it was being made functional but this was going to take some time. I have found out the time it was going to take is rather too long. Nothing apart from me being posted there has happened and it is over three years."

"So, where is the problem?"the young man asked passively.

Kalawa felt like turning him around and giving him a kick on his arse. He managed to take a deep breath, which helped calm down his nerves.

"Sir, the problem is where I'm earning a salary for work I'm not doing?"

The P.O. looked at Dr Kalawa suspiciously and asked:

"How's it a problem. You receive you salary at the end of each month, don't you?"

"Yes, I do but it's a problem because there are some people like me who feel very uncomfortable with such a situation. I want that hospital opened effectively so that I can start serving the suffering people of Karafu."

"I can now see clearly your problem. Unfortunately, the solution is not here. I'm in charge of placing doctors and other personnel of the health services. You can come back to me anytime you make up your mind."The P.O said ruefully and wished him good day.

Dr Kalawa went away wondering what the personnel officer meant by him making up his mind. 'Making up his mind about what?' he wondered. He decided to look for Pascalo to discuss his meeting with the P.O. He was advised to prepare an envelope and go back with it to the P. O. so that he would give him an appropriate posting. The situation bothered him so much but he decided to act against the dictate of his conscience. A month later he was posted to one of the referral hospitals in the city. He effectively assumed duties. Although a referral hospital, a lot of the equipment was outmoded. He felt disappointed but he was wary of complaining so he decided to try and make the best out of a bad situation. Working in bad conditions was better than not working at all.

It did not take long before the public realized how good Dr Kalawa was. His patients did so much publicity for him and his name was all over the place. Most patients who went to the hospital wanted to be consulted by Dr Kalawa only. Being an astute person, he was noting every single surgical case that he worked on. He was successful in most of them. The cases which he had not been successful had been those that were hopeless. In a space of two years in the hospital he had worked on a thousand cases. When he looked at the statistics, he realized how wasteful his time of waiting for the Karafu hospital had been.

His becoming a household name in town and in the country, did not go down well with his colleagues. Instead of generating admiration and inspiration, it rather generated hostility and animosity. Dr Kalawa was so concerned about his work that it took him a long time to notice the distaste he was generating by doing his job well and when he did his friend Pascalo was on hand for advice.

"Docta, I can see clearly that your life has changed and you're having an amazing time."

"You may be right, but there's another worry."

"You and your worries, what again?"

"I try to do my very best at work but my colleagues are not happy with me."

"Your colleagues! The nurses?"

"No, not the nurses, the doctors. None of them has a good face for me. They don't seem to appreciate the fact I'm contributing very much to the positive image of our hospital."

"I'm not surprised to hear that. Your devotion to your patients is like taking gari out of their mouths. You haven't been contaminated yet with the graft syndrome and so patients prefer you at their expense. They're bound to be angry and look at you as an obstacle in their dire effort to alleviate poverty. Now that you know, you've got to be careful where you tread."

"How would patients make them rich?"

"Good question although it betrays your naivety. Patients are desperate to get well and like every drowning person, they don't mind where they hang on for safety. Contaminated doctors take advantage of this desperation and charge huge sums of money for treatment. The patients desperately look for the money to pay for their health. You know, it is believed that health is wealth. You pay or you die, that's the sad situation. And now you come, trying to change it."

"I see what you mean but that's not what the Hippocratic oath that we all swear to upon graduation as medical doctors is all about. Money should only be incidental. I fear for the profession if things have come to this."

"Look Docta, each of us has their separate idea, which are processed and lumped up into a general idea. This general idea becomes the norm by which we live. So my brother, that's the norm. You get out of this norm, you go missing."

"My dear Pascalo, I'd rather go missing. I find it difficult to go against the bidding of my conscience."

True to himself, Dr Kalawa continued to do his job as diligently as ever, inadvertently stepping on the toes of his colleagues, some of whom were his bosses. He did the things he thought were right not bothering what the instructions from above were. This obviously got him into serious trouble - gross disrespect of hierarchy and one query after the other started coming in for him to answer. He always answered them as best as he could but everything culminated in a transfer.

Dr Kalawa assumed duties in a district hospital whose head was a GP. The GP was heading the institution by virtue of his longevity in service, so when he read the credentials of his new collaborator he became jittery even before meeting him. So when Dr Kalawa started work his boss was already putting up a front. He understood his problem and tried to make him feel at ease. Hard as he tried, success was far from coming. He then forgot about him and concentrated on the job he had been trained to do. It did not take him much time to notice that this boss of his was very popular with young girls. They were always hanging around his office, sometimes accompanied by young men. Dr Kalawa found out that their business with his boss was unholy. They were there to get their unborn babies aborted and this was what Dr Kalawa could not keep boiling in his stomach. One day he confronted him:

"Hello boss, don't you think what you're doing is illegal?"

"What do you mean? What is it I'm doing that's illegal?" asked the boss.

"Aborting pregnancies. The babies need adoption, not abortion," Dr Kalawa said blatantly.

The boss stepped two steps backwards and then took a look at Dr Kalawa for a full minute. Then his tongue loosened, releasing words that had been wrapped up in thoughts:

"I want to believe that you are here to take my exalted place. But I tell you, you can't. Do all the surgery that you can do on this earth, you will never, never be the head of this hospital. Poor you, you don't have what it takes. It will do you a lot of good if you know what it means; respect of hierarchy. If you have brains in your head, you won't question your boss' actions so blatantly. Note that whatever I do, so long as I'm boss here, is sacrosanct. So my dear Doctor Kalawa, the celebrated oncologist, you will be a better celebrity if you mind your business." he concluded, turned round and walked away.

Dr Kalawa was so confused, he did not know what to think. He simply left the spot and went back to his office where a number of patients were waiting for him. He tried to put the incident with the boss behind him in order to attend to his patients. At the end of the day he went back home and found time to think over what had happened between him and his boss. His boss had told him to mind his business if he wanted to be a better celebrity.

"Minding one's business in this case meant not interfering in the wrong doings that people around you commit," he thought. "If you see anyone stealing from another, just go along as if you've not seen what's happening or someone murdering another and you behave as if the victim deserves their fate. Where then is the virtue of being your neighbour's keeper? It all depends on conscience which Ogden Nash evaluated as follows:

There's only one way to achieve happiness on this terrestrial ball
And that is to have either a clear conscience, or none at all.

I would subscribe to a clear conscience rather than having none at all. Not having a conscience is like being unconscious, as a matter of fact dead. A world of the dead is unimaginable, so it is better to have a conscience which can be cleared in order to achieve true happiness. Being your neighbour's keeper is clearing your conscience, so we must not display indifference when we see things going wrong. We must make an effort to right them, even if, for the benefit of others – your neighbours. I would mind my business if the negative deeds of others have nothing to do with my neighbours. I wouldn't mind my business if the ethics of the profession I'm so proud of are flouted with so much impunity. I would be sorry for celebrity that is earned on the back of indifferent complacency." Concluded Dr Kalawa, as he sat down in the armchair in his office.

As he tried to relax, there was a knock on his door.

"Come in," he said feeling rather exhausted.

A woman in her late thirties walked into the office. Dr Kalawa remembered that he had made a diagnosis her before and she had a terminal illness. She was one of the nurses of the hospital but she had been on sick leave, ever since the diagnoses had been carried out.

"Yes Lulu, what can I do for you?"

"Nothing doctor. I know my time to go is near. I have for long wrestled with this illness but for some time now, I feel the verve for life ebbing away. I think that before I die I should talk to someone. Dr Kalawa, can I confide in you?" she said weakly.

"Yes, of course."

"Well, Doctor, of all doctors I've worked with, you are second only to Dr. Susuka in terms of integrity. He was such a nice person full of integrity and respect for humanity but he was flushed away like excrement in a water closet."

"Dr Susuka. I've not heard that name before."

"He was such a humble person, only his patients knew how important he was and they miss him so much." she said, tears coming out and running down her cheeks.

"So you mean he was flushed away into eternity."

"Precisely so."

"I now understand the gravity of the situation. What happened exactly?"

"That's how I come into the story. I was part of a conspiracy. He was such a likeable man but it was a paradox, his colleagues didn't like him. He was doing really well attracting the attention of the public. This, his colleagues didn't like and so they conspired to eliminate him. Poor me, because of want, I was lured to be part of the conspiracy. There was no way I could do without a conscience and so I kept it, even though it had been stained by the blood of Dr Susuka. I have longed to clear my conscience to no avail and now that I'm about to die, I fear I might meet Dr Susuku."

"What role did you play in the conspiracy?"

"I dealt him the deadly blow."

"You! How did you do it?"

"Being the nurse who was usually in attendance whenever Dr Susuka carried out an operation, it was arranged that I give him an operation mask that had been contaminated with cyanide. So on that fateful day, as he was about to operate on a patient, I prepared all the instruments and accessories that he needed, including the deadly mask. Poor doctor, as soon as he masked his mouth and nostrils, I knew that was the end of the road for him and it surely was. He later collapsed on the person he was operating upon. As soon as it happened I could see hypocrisy at its best. All the doctors rallied round the victim, running around helter-skelter to save the life they had loved to hate. An hour later Dr Susuka breathed his last and was no more and there seemed to be a cloud on every face. From that day, my conscience turned into an open wound, attracting every passing fly."

Dr Kalawa looked at Lulu intensely and thought that she deserved her dying state. He wondered how a normal human being will live with such a burden, except of course they have an obliterated conscience. He had all along wondered why a young woman like her should have been beleaguered by a malignant cancer but after her story, he knew better.

Lulu looked at Dr Kalawa with pleading eyes as if she was asking for forgiveness. The doctor understood and told her not to worry so much as she already had a terminal illness to deal with.

"Doctor," she said sorrowfully, "the terminal illness is no longer a problem for me. My problem is dying with a clear conscience, knowing that I've been forgiven of the wrong I had done to Susuka, his family, this country and the entire world."

"But you know, I'm not in a position to grant you the forgiveness you so desire."

"I know, I know, but I just need someone to sympathize with me and tell me I did something wrong but God will forgive me."

"In that case go and see a priest or a pastor."

Lulu kissed Dr Kalawa's feet and left quietly.

The Doctor was very embarrassed by the gesture but he just stood and watched Lulu go away slowly.

Dr Kalawa sat down and thought very hard. He considered option after option, wondering whether his coming home had been of any good to him. It had of course as experience is one of the best if not the best teacher. He concluded that his love for his country, if he continued to express it the way he was doing, he would surely end up like Susuka. So he decided he would express it in another way. He decided he would take a job out of the country, stay alive and examine other possibilities of being of help to his fatherland. After all it is widely believed that *he who fights and runs away, lives to fight another day.*

My Money

My imagination went riot the day I watched a fourteen-sitter bus swerve past the one in which I was an occupant. It shot in the air violently, missed its trajectory and crashed brutally against an embankment. The ensuing noise was deafening and as if that was not bad enough, it was followed by a very huge flame. Three persons managed to get out of the crashed bus but they were all aflame. What a double shock – the shock of the crash and that of the fierce fire. The rest of the occupants could not move. They had been overwhelmed by the double shock. They all succumbed to the passionate entreaties of death. Their bodies and the iron and steel that had built up the bus were in a fierce process of being charred. It was a terrible sight to behold. We fought and got the flames off the flaming bodies and then provided them with first aid treatment. It consisted of red palm oil, which we smeared on their bodies. As for the bus and the rest of its occupants, we simply watched hopelessly as it was smouldering against the road embankment. An appetite inducing smell of burnt beef was sailing gently in the air.

I was still wondering how a bus crash could cause such a huge fire, when I heard one of the three who had got out of the bus aflame moaning: oh my money, my petrol, my money. I wondered he still had enough energy to moan. I went closer to where he was lying and listened attentively. I heard the words clearly and gathered the courage to ask: "what exactly are you talking about?"

"All ma money don bon for dat motor and ma wan hundred liter petrol," he managed to say.

"For his money I could easily understand that his handbag might have been left to burn in the bus but for his one hundred litres of petrol to get burnt, I didn't quite understand. It didn't quite make sense, except that he was the vehicle owner. Even then he would have been moaning about the entire bus and not just his money and petrol. To compound my confusion, the bus was such that would have a tank whose capacity would not exceed fifty litres of petrol. So what did he mean by a hundred litres of petrol? I had to ask another onlooker who looked very agitated and terrified.

"Somtaym na businessman for zua zua na," the onlooker suggested nervously.

"Zua zua! What's that?" I asked

The man looked at me suspiciously and then said, "where yu come from sef, weh yu no know weti bi zua zua. If yu wan onli hear for ma mop, zua zua na petrol weh common pipol di sell for gallon for manage dem layf, as weh plenty small town dem and village dem no get petrol station."

The revelation unraveled the mystery that was bugging me. That ill-fated bus was also transporting containers of fuel - highly inflammable. And the police let go the risk that the driver and his passengers were taking. And here I was at a most traumatizing scene. We tried what we could do by way of help. After we had ensured that the *zua zua* man and the two others had been taken to the nearest hospital we climbed into our bus and drove off.

Two kilometres from the scene of the accident the police as usual had mounted a road block. The driver went down and settled them. One of them was good enough to throw an eye into the car and then greeted. When he did, I had the courage to ask if they were aware of the accident that had occurred two kilometres away.

"Accident," he said flatly. "Is that anything to bother about? We witness them every day and we see the victims die as they cry. So they are nothing new."

I looked at the policeman sternly, wondering whether he actually deserved the uniform he was wearing. We had left the scene of the accident without the presence of any policeman and here we were at the nearest check point to the scene and they did not care to know whether such a thing had happened, the state of the surviving victims notwithstanding.

Their concern was how much they took home at the end of the day. I remembered that at the beginning of the journey, before we completely went past the town we had gone through three checkpoints. Each time, the driver simply got out of the bus with a clenched fist and by the time he returned to the vehicle, he felt so relaxed that one would think he had just performed a very fulfilling ritual. At this check point, while I was talking to the policeman who had come to greet, the driver had *settled* (taken care of the needs of) the head of the control squad. He jumped into the bus and drove off. A few metres from the checkpoint, I asked the driver what the police and gendarmes usually checked.

"Nothing," he replied.

"Nothing?"

"No, nothing. Do you see me take any documents to them? Or do they come asking you for identification papers?"

"So, why are they at the check points?"

"To feed fat on our sweat, of course. They collect an unofficial toll from each driver at each checkpoint and that is what matters to them. Documents or no documents is no business of theirs. Safety of passengers or no safety isn't their business either."

"And they do this with so much impunity?" I asked.

"Yes, so much impunity. A goat eats where it has been tethered. It is their luck. They have been tethered where there's a lot of green grass," he said lightheartedly.

I could then understand why that bus had made all that distance with such dangerous goods in it. What a pity! The love for money has overtaken the power of love. Love for one's chosen duty to his people. I still shudder at every thought of the charred bodies and the policeman had told me it was nothing new. It did not mean anything to him and of course his colleagues. And then I remembered the day that we were flagged down by the special squad of gendarmes for traffic control. The driver had known the lack of seriousness of the squad, so he did not bother to switch off his engine. He left the bus about twenty metres from where he had been stopped, passengers and all in order to attend to the gendarmes. As they were busy negotiating, the bus started rolling forward. Before anyone could realize what was happening, it had gathered speed and was going down a slope with no driver behind the steering wheel. Unfortunately, the passengers at the front seats were both women and all they could do was shout: Jesus! Jesus! Jesus! Suddenly there was total commotion in the bus as passengers put up a desperate fight against death as they saw it coming. Fortunately, there was a house between the speeding bus and the valley it was heading to. It crashed into the house breaking a wall which stood as a wedge. The bus stopped and the rest of the passengers who were still inside got out. The driver ran to the scene with his hands on his head blaming everyone but himself and his gendarme friends. He wondered why no-one had the presence of mind to press their foot on the brakes to stop the car. The gendarmes did not even bother to come to the scene. Instead, the driver went back to them to confirm what they had witnessed twenty metres away. They simply asked the driver to wait for the owner of the house so as to arrange amicably. The house owner who was a peasant farmer had gone to his farm. We all had to wait for his return. We were fortunate he came back two hours later. As soon as he saw the scene, he started shouting, oh my money, my money and rushed into the house entering one of the rooms that was covered by the broken wall. After a while, he returned feeling relieved. He then went into negotiations with the driver and they arrived at an arrangement. The bus was then pulled back to the road, the damage on it was not very serious. All the passengers climbed in and once again they were en route.

Passengers are usually treated to all kinds of scenarios as they use public transport. There was this day that a driver was stopped at one of the checkpoints and he went off his car furiously, shouting "what again? I've already given my contribution for the day." The aggression of the policeman suddenly changed. He was the one who calmed down the driver, took him aside and their scores were settled. When the driver got back to the steering wheel, he was all cursing: "what kind of bad luck is this. Look at his fat stomach. He thinks he should use me to prepare for his retirement. It's hardly two hours since I passed through this check point and gave these people my own contribution of three thousand francs which allows me to use the road for the day, without being molested. And then I come not long after and he has the guts to blow his stupid whistle. Of what use was my money then? May the prince of darkness descend on him. It's a curse to be a policeman or any of these bribe-taking uniformed men and women. I swear that I shall disown any of my children who show interest in such a job. Thank God the children themselves travel and see how disgraceful they are."

The driver continued to grumble and curse inaudibly. By the time his temperament settled down, he was at another check point. There he was well received.

"Paddy man, is this your coming?" the police officer asked.

"Yes pa it's my coming."

"I hope your passengers are in order."

"Of course pa. Every single passenger is in order."

Just as he was about to wave the driver off, he noticed a young man sitting behind the driver. Instinctively he spoke to him.

"My friend, let me see your I.D card."

"Here you are," the young man said handing him a piece of paper.

"What's this?"the policeman asked.

"As you can see, it's an attestation of loss."

The policeman looked at the document carefully, as he did so another young man who sat next to me and holding one of the balls made from coagulated latex became jittery. The policeman examined the face of the young man whose document he was holding, and then ordered him to get out of the car. The young man protested.

"But that's a valid document duly stamped and signed by a police commissioner."

"I know but get out of the car," the policeman insisted.

At this point the driver intervened, "but pa officer what's going on? I thought I had told you all my passengers were in order?"

"Paddy man, this one isn't and there may be others, only I don't have time to check them now. I have to deal with the present situation."

"How is he not in order? Has his attestation of loss expired?"

"No, but his case is special. No right thinking policeman will sign an attestation of loss of a resident permit. He's an immigrant who claims he has lost his resident permit and has been issued an attestation of loss. My friend, I'll not be the one to be fooled."

"I'm not fooling you. Don't you see on the document the name of the commissioner who established it? You can contact him. He's your colleague after all."

"My dear friend, stop running your mouth. You are in deep trouble. You'll have to be locked up. If an immigrant like you loses a resident permit anytime, a temporary one is issued immediately. There's no question of an attestation of loss. Do you understand?"

"But oga officer, try to understand my problem. I paid some money for the attestation to be established. I didn't know it was not valid."

"Boy, you don't seem to understand the gravity of your crime. Right now you're an illegal immigrant and what that amounts to is immediate deportation. Take him and lock him up in our temporary cell."

The young man's bag was taken out of the car and he was being led to a make-shift cell. Fellow passengers were urging him to settle them and the boy took out ten thousand francs out of his pocket and offered it to the policeman. He looked at it and shook his head in the negative. The young man finally got to the cell. He was fortunate the rest of the passengers understood the situation and some of them along with the driver, went to negotiate for his release. After ten minutes he returned to the car and his mighty problems were over. Again the driver started ranting:

"You these immigrants, you think you're so clever. You have a problem like this and you don't warn the driver in advance so he can know what to do at checkpoints. See how much time it has taken us at the place. What you should know is that on days like this that the ship will take off from the harbour, uniform officers know it will be windfall for them from anyone who has the misfortune of being a trader, immigrants and nationals alike."

As we drove on to our destination I understood why many civil servants are still up to the task of taking care of their families and also afford to drink, and entertain guests with, beer.

By the time we got to journey's end , I had been obliged to change all my plans for the evening. The journey had taken twice the usual time.

I was waiting for the young man with the ball made from coagulated latex to get out so that I too could do same but instead he sat there looking worried

"What's the problem young man?" I asked.

"Big problem! I can't find that my ball," he said desperately.

"The ball in raw coagulated latex?"

"Exactly!"

"Is that something you should disturb yourself and other people about? Give me way," I said feeling frustrated.

He shifted his legs to the left and I got out. He remained in the car moaning, "my money oh my money."

"Did I hear well," I wondered.

The moaning turned into weeping and I heard clearly. He was actually weeping for his money.

"What money are you weeping about?" I dared ask.

"All my money," he replied in tears.

"What do you mean? All your money," I asked confused.

"Yes, all the money, I had to cross the border with. I had put it in that ball. Now that it's missing, I too I'm missing," he said with a resigned look.

"You can't be serious. Nobody gets missing because of money."

"Well," the young man said, "today you're standing in front of one such person. There's no way I can pick up my life again. I was supposed to do some good business with the money had I succeeded in crossing with it. Now I'm completely lost. The money's lost in that ball."

I looked at the young man and pitied him. From every indication he was one of the immigrants trading across one of our borders. To beat our bribery-happy policemen he had resorted to carting away his money cash in inflated balls — what ingenuity! He was on his way to board the ship at the harbor.

64

Pastor Aduma's Concubine

Pastor Aduma had sworn that he would leave the church if his subsequent post were not a juicy one. When he joined God's ministry in 1999, it was to serve God and also make some money to get himself and his family out of the spell of poverty. He and his family had known poverty ever since he was born and when he became an adult he thought he could marry a girl in his neighbourhood but as soon as he mentioned the issue, the girl retorted, ' how can one add poverty onto poverty?' When Pastor Aduma wondered at what she meant, she explained that she came from a poor family, so she could not possibly marry someone from another poor family. Pastor Aduma was so devastated by the response that when he got back home he could not help asking his father why they were so poor.

'Son,' the old man said, 'the spell of poverty had been cast on us. There's no way we can get out of it.'

'Yes father. We can. We can get out of it,' the young man said confidently.

The following month he had admission into a theological college. He had not had any secondary education but by dint of hard work, he had written and passed both the ordinary and advanced level General Certificate of Education examinations. He grew up to be a fine singer and so featured prominently in the Chimers Choir. Just before he entered the theological college, he had assumed the leadership role of the choir. He was dark, slim and tall. He wore a permanent smile on his face and people usually wondered whether he could ever be angry.

When he got out of the School of Theology and was ordained pastor, he had the luck to have been posted to a prominent parish in the city as an associate pastor. He soon established himself as a man of God, highly respected by his parishioners. It didn't take him long to find a wife and his faith in God, for whom he was a servant, was growing steadily. One weekend, the main pastor had left for his village to participate in development and cultural activities there. Meanwhile, back in the city a very prominent man from a prominent family had died and his burial had been scheduled for that weekend. When members of the prominent family got to the prominent parish to arrange for the prominent man's funeral, they found the associate pastor.

'Pastor, we're here to make arrangements for a requiem mass in honour of our late father.'

'That should be no trouble. May I have his membership card?'

'Here you are.'

'I'm afraid this card had expired five years ago. Why had the old man not renewed his membership?'

'He had been ill.'

'I'm sure not ill enough to forget sending one of his children to come and renew his membership. Is there anyone of you who is regular?'

'It depends on what you mean by regular. We all are baptized Christians.'

'Do you have up-to-date membership cards?'

They all looked embarrassed and confessed that the last time the most regular of them went to church was three years ago. Pastor Aduma told them that he was sorry he could not help them because he didn't want to encourage backsliding among Christians.

The family went away disappointed but not discouraged. They decided to meet one of the church elders. He was the most senior elder of the parish. He went on to meet Pastor Aduma on behalf of the prominent family.

66

'Pastor Aduma, I hear you've rejected family Akonji's request for a requiem mass for their late father?'

'Yes of course. They don't meet the requirements,' the pastor replied.

'What requirements?'

'You should know them elder. The late man isn't a communicant nor was he regular in paying up his church contributions.'

'How much does he owe?' the elder asked.

'Depends on how much he was capable of paying annually. The church is not there to assess people's incomes in order to attribute a percentage for God's work. It's left for the Christian to rely on their conscience and pay their contributions accordingly. For five years Pa Akonji hadn't paid anything. So he didn't even have the will to pay,' pastor Aduma said.

'I'm insisting on this matter because this family is very rich and they are prepared to pay anything to ensure their father's salvation,' the elder said persuasively.

'If one's salvation depends on a requiem mass then people should learn to meet their church obligations when they are alive. It's absolutely ridiculous for church contributions to be paid post-humously,' Pastor Aduma insisted.

'I do agree with you pastor but I'd like that you bend the rule in this case. Pa Akonji is a man we all know. He might have had his reasons for failing to contribute for the progress of the church in the last five years but then he's been surprised by death and his children wish to offer him a funeral that befits his status here on earth and also ensure that he has a place in heaven,' the elder said.

'Unfortunately elder, unfortunately,' the pastor insisted, 'all the members of pa Akonji's family are backsliders. There's none who's even a regular church-goer. I don't think there's anything we can do for them.'

There's something you can do pastor Aduma. I strongly believe that if the main pastor were here he would have found a solution. So you too can find a solution pastor.'

'Which I had long ago."

'Great to hear that. What have you resolved to do?'

'Send them away of course. Let them do whatever they want to do with their father's corpse, keeping the church out of it.'

'Pastor,' said the elder that's not the kind of solution I yearn to hear. What you don't seem to understand is that this funeral is going to be a big crowd puller. Not just any big crowd but the cream of this country, who will come from all over. Also think of the offerings these people will make. The church, our church will stand to gain. Make no mistake pastor,' the elder said looking at the pastor intently.

The pastor was lost for words. He simply stood looking as vulnerable as a motherless lamb.

The church bells tolled dolefully and minutes later, a procession intoned a dirge. The churchyard was full of cars of all makes, shapes and sizes. The mourners were so elegantly dressed a stranger would think they were celebrants. They filed into the church carefully selecting where to sit. Each one of them held an impeccably white handkerchief to dust their seat before they put their buttocks on it. Everyone solemnly stood when the hearse was ushered into the church, signaling the beginning of the requiem mass.

When the mass ended and the casket had been taken away for internment, some church officials stayed back to count the cash that had come in as funeral offerings. Much of the money was in maximum notes of ten thousand francs. Shortly after the internment, pastor Aduma got back to the church premises, anxious to know how much had been collected. When the total was announced, his eyes shown like a torch newly fed with two pairs of batteries. Over four million francs, collected in a single funeral service sounded like a distant dream. The pastor looked at the pile of notes and then the heap of coins gleefully and started the arduous task of a recount. By the time the last coin was thrown on the heap it was exactly four million four hundred and forty francs. He sent for a representative of the bereaved family. When he came he took him aside and presented the money to him. The representative said they had nothing to do with it. All they were interested in was to have their father's corpse blessed and prayed for in God's house. Whatever had been collected was at the disposal of the presiding pastor. He left the pastor dumbfounded.

Pastor Aduma was all by himself, facing a pile and a heap of money. He wondered whether it was for real. He felt around him and confirmed that it was for real. 'This is something!' he exclaimed, 'in one fell swoop, I'm the sole owner of over four million francs. God's actually riding high. He's great. Somehow, I've been dreaming of riding a personal car without having an inkling of how it would come about. Here am I in the threshold of that car. I'm going to ride a car without going on my knees to appeal to the congregation to send round a special basket, every Sunday for the acquisition of the pastor's car. I think I'm greatly blessed,' pastor Aduma said gratefully and left for his home to keep his money. He stuffed his pockets with a hundred thousand francs and left for the church elder's house. On his way, he bought him a gift. When the elder saw him he exclaimed:

'Man-of-God! What's brought you to my doorsteps?'

'Joy has brought me here. I'm overjoyed by the fruits I've reaped at the requiem mass. Remember it was through your persuasion that I accepted to preside over the mass. So I've come to spill over some of my joy on you. The bereaved family has decided to leave everything that had been harvested with me. And you know what was harvested wasn't child's play. I've never known such generosity in my life. In my own small way I've come to demonstrate my appreciation of the role you played in the whole thing. This is a large bottle of Chivas, have it from me. It's the first time I've ever offered a gift like this.'

'Man-of-God, honestly I did what I did for the old man and not to help you. I thought he deserved a befitting burial and he had it. That was what mattered to me. You don't need to thank me for anything'

'Yes, I need to. You've made me understand that there can be money in God's ministry. Have the gift. I give it to you with all my heart. It shall please me exceedingly if you accept it.'

'All right, I do accept it. Thank you very much pastor.'

'You're welcome elder,' pastor Aduma said, feeling very satisfied.

Before the main pastor of the parish came back from his trip, pastor Aduma had bought himself a white Toyota Tercel, station wagon model. It was very fulfilling for him as he could transport himself in comfort and at his convenience. It was an unpleasant surprise for the main pastor of the parish when he returned. Pastor Aduma, his associate was the last person he expected to have a car. The congregation had barely struggled to buy one for him and it was going to take a very long time for a second one to be bought for the associate pastor. Shortly after, he got information about the money that had rained on his church in his absence. He was visibly bitter that it had happened in such an inauspicious moment. Current immediately stopped flowing between him and his associate. It was therefore no surprise that six months later, Pastor Aduma was transferred to another parish. It was in a village that was situated one hundred kilometres north of the city. The name was Kukwa and it had only sixty regular worshippers. When pastor Aduma got there he found out that even though the church house had corrugated iron sheets as roof, the manse was a thatch house. When he drove in his car, the entire village got very excited. It was the first time they had seen a pastor who owned a car and they wondered how he would live in a thatch house. Pastor Aduma had no choice. He and his Christians soon got used to having with them a car owner who lived in a thatch house. Pastor Aduma's car turned out to be very useful in the village as it was used to transport a number of emergency health cases to the city for medical attention. The difficulty was in maintenance and fuelling. The pastor's finances were dwindling very fast because his new parish was not only small but also very poor to be of help to itself and its parish pastor. So gradually it became very painful to run the car. The pastor had to do everything to adapt to the situation. He eventually sold the car and bought a motorbike. This equally facilitated his movements and was relatively cheaper to run. The bike had an added advantage in that during the rainy seasons the roads became passable only for people on foot or on bikes.

In the long run, pastor Aduma viewed his transfer as a sort of punishment inflicted on him. He saw clearly why some postings were preferred to others. He had always thought that in the service of God pastors should be sent anywhere and they should go without complaining embracing the joys and hardships. But his experience in Kukwa had made him realize that he had to apply to leave the place, otherwise he would be there all his life. Three years had gone by and there was no hope of him being transferred. He grew fond of the people and became more committed in their community activities. This even helped him to win more converts into Christianity. One of his new converts was a young woman called Mary. Pastor Aduma used to wonder how she got the name Mary whereas she was not a Christian. She later explained: 'when a school was established in Kukwa, the first teachers who came insisted on English names. Whenever you came to register and gave your name, they insisted that you must also give them an English name. So on the spot someone had to think out an English name for you. Mine was Mary and I didn't even know what it meant or stood for. It was later in my life that the import of the name dawned on me'.

She had been in school for four years and she dropped out when her father died. She dropped out to assist her mother raise her two younger brothers and three sisters. The pastor was easily welcomed into the home and soon became the wonderful counselor of the household.

Mary was such a young woman whose appearance could not be ignored. She was smoothly fair-coloured with a not-so-broad nose beautifully placed between her two attractive cheeks that had the grace of dimples. She walked upright with steps as graceful as those of a lioness. At eighteen, she was one metre seventy-three centimetres tall. Her voice was a potential asset to the Chimers Choir, which pastor Aduma had just set up in Kukwa. Service was a good attraction for pastor Aduma to Mary's household but Mary herself was even a greater attraction. She easily became the light that shone in the pastor's ministry in the village of Kukwa. He no longer bothered whether he was transferred from Kukwa or not. His complaints were fast assuming diminishing returns. Shortly after, wherever the pastor went Mary was behind his bike. Mama pastor, so the pastor's wife was fondly called, believed so much in her husband that she told everyone who cared to listen that Adu was simply shepherding a lost lamb. She was as caring as her namesake, Elizabeth who later became the mother of John the Baptist.

A strange coincidence eventually occurred in Kukwa. Mama pastor and Mary the lost lamb were found to be pregnant at the same time. For both it was their first pregnancy. Mama pastor had been praying hard to have a baby. After four years of marriage, she had almost given up that she would one day have a baby. Pastor Aduma had persistently told her not to worry, impressing on her that

God's time was the best. And in fact she felt like an angel when she realized she was pregnant, forgiving any wrong that had been meted on her or was being meted. In that situation she embraced Mary as a sister even after she had understood that her unborn child will be born an Aduma. Two Aduma babies were expected and the beauty of it all was that the two women who carried the babies loved each other so much. Mary had moved in and together they cooked for the pastor. Together they sang in the pastor's choir and together they watched the pastor's congregation grow. The pastor turned out to be a happy man. Never has man seen such friendship that a woman agrees to share her home with a concubine. The villagers watched in amazement, considering that the pastor had always told them about the merits of monogamy and had never admitted anyone with two or more wives in his church. They decided to wait and see. The pastor was doing well as more and more villagers found him likeable and joined his church. He had created a farm in the village and encouraged his Christians to work as a common initiative group that collectively develop farms for individuals. This was found to be wonderful and many young boys and girls of Kukwa swelled the benches of the church.

It had just rained and the dust in Kukwa had settled. A cool breeze was breezing softly into Pastor Aduma's house. He had improved on it renewing the thatches to prevent any leakages. He had also created two more bedrooms. One for Mary and the other for himself. The existing bedroom was left for Elizabeth alias Mama pastor. The pastor had left earlier in the day to carry out pastoral work and at six p.m. he had not returned.

'Ma-ma P. come o, I feel a sharp pain in my womb,' shouted Mary.

'I feel exactly the same thing,' Mama pastor cried out.

And soon after, both women were screaming. They were immediately taken to the village health centre and the midwife was summoned. One hour later each of the women was delivered of a baby boy. They looked so much alike, one would take them for identical twins. This time it was no coincidence. It only proved whom their father was- Pastor Aduma, the first human being to produce a pair of identical twins with two different women. When he got to the health centre he could not open his eyes wider. He embraced and kissed each of the women passionately. He named Mary's son Emmanuel and Elizabeth's John.

The children were such an attraction and brought about more love between the two mothers. They usually got confused which of the boys was John and which, Emmanuel. The confusion did not bother them as they treated both children like theirs. The two women developed their singing skills and they became outstanding in music. Pastor Aduma encouraged them and they did not only belong to the Chimers Choir but with the initiative of the pastor they created the Fantastic Trio. They sang so well and they were told they would do even better when they move to a city parish where things were juicy. It was at this point that Pastor Adamu started insisting on being transferred to a parish where he and his women would make better use of their talents in spreading Christ's message. Three consecutive years he had applied for transfer and three consecutive years his application had been turned down. It was when he applied the fourth time that he had vowed to leave the church if his application was not given due consideration. And indeed the consideration was not due. Pastor Aduma became confrontational and moved to the higher quarters of the church to find out why they had decided to bury him in Kukwa. The head of the church answered:

'You should rather be happy. For a rolling stone gathers no moss. We've observed you've gathered and are still gathering a lot of moss.'

'Why should that apply only to me. Almost ten years in a parish is too much. I want to leave and I must.'

'If you must, then leave, let's see. Young man you can't come here and intimidate your bosses'

'It's not my intention to intimidate anybody, only I've been pushed to the wall'.

'Ah you've been pushed to the wall. I thought it was rather the church that had been pushed to the wall,' the head of the church said cynically.

'The church, pushed to the wall. How do you mean?'

'Pastor Aduma, there're certain things which the church prefers to be quiet about. That's why we've been silent all these years. If you didn't know it, you are a disgrace to those of us who work in the Lord's vineyard. We've slept over this matter for a very long time and today you've provoked it. Is it right for a servant of the Lord to live in adultery? As a matter of fact have a concubine? You've done so well to keep us out of it but remember the flock you shepherd are human beings with brain. We're aware of the marvelous work you're doing in Kukwa. We're especially aware of the angelic voices you've nurtured and the role they play in winning souls for the church. We're aware that both your wife and concubine live happily together in the manse, how you did it must have required a lot of skill. So, we thought you had better stay where you are,' he said looking at Pastor Aduma searchingly.

'Stay where I am bringing salvation to other people whereas I'm in dire need of it myself,' Pastor Aduma said and walked out on the head of his church.

The Wound of Justice

Toki Joe had always admired the law. So it was no surprise that at fifteen, he used to go to court premises during holidays, only to admire lawyers and judges in their professional outfit. Sometimes he attended court sessions. In one of them the presiding magistrate made a statement that caught his attention. The magistrate was addressing a criminal: you seem to have so much respect for the truth that you use it sparingly. Toki Joe thought it was paradoxical that you can respect something and then be afraid to use it. It should be like all God-fearing people, who have so much respect for the Lord their God that they call His name and on Him several times a day. Later in life Toki Joe re-examined the statement within the context of awe. When you're in awe of someone or any entity, you call its name sparingly. The judge actually meant to say that the criminal was a liar. Liars understandably have little to do with the truth.

Another statement that made so much impression on him was one made by Benjamin Disraeli, a one-time British Prime Minister, in one of his speeches: *Justice is truth in action*. His interpretation of this statement was that any justice done to anyone is based on truth and nothing but the truth. It became a guiding principle in his life and so he went on to study law. After graduation he had preferred the bench to the bar. He rose in the profession to become a court of appeal judge, which rewarded him with the title Justice. This title was appended to his name and soon after he was known as Justice Toki Joe. Some people went to the extent of adding honourable to it.

77

Justice Toki, was not particularly popular among people who thought that they could arm-twist justice. He was said to be *unnecessarily* strict. Most People within his jurisdiction thought that he was not a flexible judge. There was this case of a sub-divisional officer who had defiled and impregnated a minor of fifteen. The parents made a complaint to the appropriate quarters, to the effect that their daughter-a minor, had been abused by the Divisional Officer, which was aggravated by persistent sexual relations with her. They eventually sued and claimed damages for the prejudice suffered as a result. Not being satisfied with the judgment of the lower court, they lodged an appeal against it. Justice Toki Joe happened to be the president of the panel on appeal. The sub-divisional officer had used his position to influence the judgment at the lower court to be in his favour and he thought he would do the same at the higher court. After all, Justice Toki had been his classmate at secondary school. He decided to visit him before the case came up for hearing.

When he knocked and entered, Justice Toki smiled and exclaimed:

"Jesco Jesco! What a coincidence! I was just going through your case file and here you are."

"Here am I indeed. I was coming to see you just for that. You see, this our job of working with the rural population is rather daunting and dishonourable. People think they can get rich on our backs by setting all types of traps and pushing us to fall in them. That's what they have done to me recently but thank God, *justice is truth in action*. They've seen the truth in action but they don't want to believe and so they've taken an appeal. Unfortunately for them, the appeal is going to be handled by my own friend, Toki Joe, Toki the law."

"You need not worry, Jesco the jester, turned, *chef de terre*, you've said it all my dear friend, Justice is truth in action indeed. If the evidence is nothing but the truth, then justice will prevail" said Justice Toki Joe.

"I count on you. I count very much on you", said the sub-divisional officer stepping out of the judge's chambers.

When Jesco left, Toki Joe picked up the case file involving him and examined it carefully. To his greatest dismay, he found out that justice had been literally butchered at the lower court. Ample evidence had been tendered to show that the fifteen-year-old victim, a form two girl in a local secondary school had, following her relationship with Jesco, been irregular at school, eventually got pregnant and dropped out of school. Jesco had, in the presence of witnesses, admitted in writing, his responsibility and even proposed a sum of money to keep their mouths shot. Although this evidence proved their case beyond reasonable doubt, the judge of the lower court found him not guilty on the grounds that Jesco was a gentleman, known by all to be so, and had signed the document admitting responsibility as a relief to the poor parents of the girl, and therefore discharged and acquitted him.

Justice Toki could not conjecture how Jesco had gone scot free. He reviewed the entire case and found his friend Jesco guilty of the offence and therefore liable to pay the family of the victim full damages. He wondered how justice had been truth in action in Jesco's case. Something might have gone wrong somewhere. He and Jesco had been classmates for five years and throughout that period he had been known as the Jester. He always made people laugh but somehow he also made them brood. He remembered how Jesco had invited a girl in the neighbourhood of the college campus and taken her to the dormitory. The rest of the students were doing sports that afternoon on the playground. Jesco was rather having fun with his unwelcome visitor. Luck ran against them when the warden was passing by and talking to someone across the block. As soon as he heard his voice, he requested the girl to go under another student's bed. He asked her to pretend to be deaf and dumb. As soon as the girl had tucked herself under the bed, he tiptoed to one of the back windows, opened it carefully and jumped out. Unfortunately, the window closed with a bang and this attracted the attention of the warden. He opened the closed door and looked in. He found only the emptiness of the room. Six beds occupying each of the two rows. He wondered what might have caused the bang and his eyes fell on the loose shutter. He went to the window and shut the shutter tightly. He walked back to the door. Just as he was about to close it the girl under the bed breathed heavily. This again attracted the warden's attention. He directed his eyes under the bed where the sound had come from. He saw a protruding leg and was sure something unusual was happening. He went to the bed. He stooped and held the leg and tugged it. The girl squeezed herself out and stood up. The warden was very surprised.

"What are you doing here?" the warden asked.

The girl almost reacted but he remembered that Jesco had asked her to pretend to be dumb and deaf. So, she only stood, looking at him stupidly.

"I'm talking to you. What are you doing here?" the warden pursued.

Still, there was no answer. The warden made several attempts to make the young girl speak but to no avail. So he concluded that she was deaf. He then got the name of the boy under whose bed she was hiding and summoned him to his office.

Unfortunately, the boy had no idea of what the warden was talking about nor did he know anything about the girl who had been shown to her. All the other members of the room including Jesco had been summoned but the problem could not be solved. The girl seemed to have come from nowhere but she must have been up for something, somehow, somewhere. The college was for boys only, so if a girl, even if she were deaf and dumb, went missing in one of the dormitories, she must be up for some pranks. The warden, after having failed to get anything out of the girl and because he did not want to get the villagers meddle in college problems he let her go. He however decided to get the twelve occupants of the room severely punished.

It was after the punishment had been carried out that Jesco explained to his roommates what had happened. They understandably did not find his story funny at all, but they all decided not to give it any importance. Since then Joki had always had his misgivings about Jesco's future. Even when he eventually became a civil administrator, he had his doubts. And true to what he had always thought of him, Jesco had taken advantage of his position to disadvantage a vulnerable rural family.

On the day of the case, Justice Toki gave it a fair hearing. First the prosecution made its submission. The learned counsel observed that there was a total miscarriage of justice at the lower court. From the evidence adduced in the evidence produced, it was clear that Jesco had entertained sexual relationship with a minor of fifteen. This is evident in the fact that she got pregnant and dropped out of school. Jesco himself had signed a recognisant to bear the cost of the pregnancy and delivery. Under section 346, subsection 1 and 3 of the penal code states amongst others that any act of indecency to a minor is punishable by law. This is aggravated by any sexual intercourse between the minor and the offender, notwithstanding the minor's consent. The learned counsel concluded that Jesco be given a maximum sentence.

The defence counsel on his part took the floor in an effort to flaw the arguments of the prosecutor. He argued that the young girl was not a minor, considering that her birth certificate had been established on the basis of a sworn affidavit. Such affidavits were mere declarations which most of the time were false. It takes only a bottle of beer to motivate some-one, anyone at all to go to a court and declare your age for you. Sometimes, the person declaring is younger than you. He then harped on the fact that the was tall and huge, and also good enough to be anybody's wife. She actually looked like a girl who could beat up a man, her chest as broad as wrestler's. He implored the learned judge to have a closer look at the girl and determine whether she was still a miner. On the grounds of his arguments he requested the learned judge to uphold the judgement of the lower court. He went on to urge him to ignore the recognisant to bear the cost of the pregnancy and eventual delivery, saying that the document had been signed out of pity for the family, whose level of poverty was so low that they could send out their teenage daughters to prostitute for their welfare. Jesco, being a very kind hearted person easily took pity on the family and personally undertook to alleviate them from such extreme poverty. "Why then should a man like that be punished?" the defence counsel pondered. "My lord!" he exclaimed "I trust that you will give justice a chance by not letting rustics take advantage of the saintly heart of a well-meaning civil administrator and ruin a career which he has so brilliantly laid a solid foundation."

The learned lawyer sat down officiously. He pulled out a white handkerchief from his side pocket and wiped off the sweat on his face. He looked round the court room satisfied that he had done a good job.

Without wasting time, the learned judge gave his ruling as follows. In the absence of any other birth certificate, there is no doubt that the young girl is a minor. Considering this fact, it is undoubtedly appalling a man of Jesco's standing, a man who is supposed to be a role model for the youth, should go so low as to entertain a sexual relationship with a so-called rustic, her young age notwithstanding. The law will be undoing itself if it allows perpetrators of such acts go scot free. That said, for the sake of the unborn child, I shall tamper justice with mercy by giving Mr Jesco a six-months suspended sentence and a fine of two million CFA to be paid as damages to the aggrieved family. May the court rise.

Jesco stood up with a heavy heart, not believing what he had just experienced. He could not understand why his own classmate had to be so hard on him. He had barely missed going to prison and invariably losing his job. He thought deeply and wondered whether he should go and say 'thank you' to his friend and classmate Justice Toki. He shook his head and thought aloud : 'no the learned judge has not done me any justice. True he had tampered justice with mercy in his judgement but he had said it clearly himself, it was for the sake of the unborn child, not for my sake. Our friendship doesn't mean anything to him. I wonder whether he actually lives and operates in this our country where the right connection is everything. I remember a case that was worse than mine. A well respected person had impregnated a minor and had given her money to abort the baby in order to avoid any scandal. But a worse scandal emerged as the teenager lost her life in the attempt to abort the baby. The matter initially raised hell but as the investigations progressed, the gravity of the crime regressed. In the final analysis, the case files disappeared and the well respected man still goes about with his head high. Many of such cases abound, some as serious as highhanded murder. The latest case was that which came up a week before. A responsible person in charge of one of the state treasuries had looted it of a whooping one and half billion francs. The case was in court and everyone had expected that the criminal would receive a grave jail term. But to everyone's chagrin the man was discharged and acquitted. The question on the lips of many was 'what was his secret?'

His secret was that he had acquired what mattered. And to many, what matters is money. With some bank safes stacked with a whooping one and half billion francs that belonged to him, it was only in a very exceptional case like Justice Toki, that he would be unable to buy justice. So that was his secret. He had bought over every single person that had to do with the case with sums ranging from a thousand francs to tens of millions. Money, no matter how it was acquired is the magic key that opens every door. At this point it dawned on Jesco that he had not given Justice Toki anything and he had not even tried to do so.

'What would have been his reaction?' he asked himself.

Jesco's attempt to find an answer did not yield immediate fruits. So he gave up and decided to accept his sentence, thanking God for his generous mercies because it could have been worse.

Brown Kaloka the Coxcomb

Brown Kaloka is a young man in his late thirties. He has a height of one and half metre, which many people consider as average. But he has always wished he was taller. So he has adopted the habit of always raising his shoulders to satisfy himself that he is tall enough. Another characteristic is that his face is rather spherical but he had wished it to be shaped like a V. In order to satisfy this gnawing wish, he adopted a haircut that rather flattened his hair and made it look like a plateau. Fortunately, the almighty God had endowed him with so much hair, so his barber could easily shape it the way he wanted. This hairstyle, he called it coxcomb, which later earned him his nickname. Many people who knew him started referring to him as Brown Kaloka, the coxcomb. Incidentally, like any coxcomb, Brown Kaloka is particularly concerned about his clothes. Ever since he got out of the depth of poverty, his clothing has been specially ordered from well-known designers.

He had always counted himself as lucky when he went to the training school that trained customs officers. He said it was a very competitive exercise to gain admission, especially financially. The financial requirement, though subtle, was one million francs and he had to press on his poverty-stricken parents to do everything to make the money available. So they did, after a lot of gymnastics. Once in the school the coxcomb couldn't wait to graduate. He always told whoever could listen that he had had his own fair share of poverty and that as soon as he left school he would do everything in his power to catch up with affluence. So when he left school he knew exactly what to do.

85

His first post was at the country's only seaport. He was in charge of all goods entering the country whether for sale or for personal use. He took advantage of the loose system of customs revenue collection, which was not even computerized, to make enormous wealth for himself. He once boasted publicly that the government of the people was actually for people like him. He went on to say that he was being paid a monthly salary to make money for himself, claiming that for every billion francs that went to the government treasury from the port, half a billion went into his personal account. So it had hardly taken him six months on his job to catch up with an affluent lifestyle. Unfortunately, the plans he had had for his dear father, who had made enormous sacrifice for his education could not materialise. The old man died of a malignant cancer before it was properly diagnosed. Coxcomb decided that celebrations marking his father's death would have to reflect the kind of money his son has. The first thing he thought of doing was to put the corpse in a reliable mortuary. He was afraid that with the frequent power failure in the country no local mortuary would be able to preserve his father's corpse properly. So he had to arrange for a special flight to Switzerland to take his father's corpse there. This done, he embarked on building a mansion in Kitchati, his village. He requested an architect to design and produce a plan for him. When he went to pick it up, the architect was about to attend to another client but he went out of his way to fish out the plan and presented to him. After the architect's hasty explanations he looked at him condescendingly and asked:

'How much will this cost?'

'About fifty million francs CFA,' the architect answered dryly.

'What?' Brown Kaloka asked raising his voice.

'It could be less. It's only an estimate,'

'Less?'

'Less, as I said earlier, it's only an estimate. Estimates are usually made with positive cost margins. So that amount shouldn't scare you,' the architect said soothingly.

'Scare me you say!' Brown almost shouted.

'Er Mr Kaloka. I don't understand anymore. Would you excuse me I've got to attend to other clients, who have been waiting impatiently.'

'I can see we don't understand one another. You see, I'm a very, very rich man. My worth is in billions, not even in millions. Tell me how much those clients of yours are going to pay you and I'll pay and let you attend to me until I'm satisfied,' he said bluffing.

The architect took a good look at him and then requested him to sit down. He went out for five minutes, during which he negotiated with the other clients for another appointment. When he returned, he found Mr Kaloka waiting impatiently.

'Yes Mr Emens, You appear not to know my worth. I'm not the kind of person to carry out a building project for fifty million francs. The least cost I expected of the project had to be ten times the costing you have just presented to me. So you've got to go back to your drawing board. Actually I want something very good. I want my father's corpse to be laid in a fantastic mansion. Even if it costs two billion francs,' he said proudly.

'Don't blame me sir. I was doing an estimate for the *Chef de Bureau* I know. Now that you talk only in terms of billions, I've got to change my mind,' the architect said apologetically.

'You had better do. Sometimes you shouldn't trust what you know. I may be only a chief clerk but mind you, no goods leave the port without my powerful signature. Actually, almost all of the import and export trade in this country depends on that signature, which is mine. So you see, Mr Emens, it's sometimes dangerous to undermine anyone before you know them very well'

'I'll go back to the drawing board as suggested,' the architect said and excused himself.

Mr Emens shook his head sadly wondering how a civil servant who had not even worked for a year could be so boastful about money. When the estimate he had previously worked on had come up to fifty million francs, he had wondered where Brown Kaloka was going to find all that money. Paradoxically he claims it had been an effrontery to associate him with such a small amount of money. He even claimed a project of two billion francs wouldn't be a bother to him. 'Yes, money talks,' Mr Emens said sadly.

He went back to the drawing board and designed a mansion that was costed at a billion francs. Two days after, he handed the plan to the Coxcomb. He looked at it and nodded with satisfaction. He unzipped his briefcase and took out a wad of notes. He settled his bill cash – a hundred million francs as it turned out to be. Ever since he opened his firm, Mr Emens had never received such a huge amount of payment at a go. He felt very excited but embarrassed that a man who depends on the taxpayers money could pay him that much. He simply shrugged his shoulders and whistled home to meet his wife and two kids.

Mr Brown Kaloka, the Coxcomb took his plan to a famous construction company, called Eight International. After a careful study of the plan a contract was signed and the next day, he and the General Manager of the company travelled to Kitchati, where the project was to be executed. For the first time, the G.M of Eight International travelled on a road where there were no bridges. Their four-wheel-drive Toyota Hilux had to swim through rivers and streams. By the time they got to Kitchati, the G.M was already wondering whether the contract was worth the trouble. When he made his worries known, the Coxcomb on the spot offered him another contract to build bridges and improve on the road to Kitchati. The Coxcomb was only too glad that this would be done before his father's burial. Money was no obstacle to any of his projects. As soon as they returned to the city, another contract was prepared and signed. It was to cost another two billion francs, considering that three bridges had to be constructed. This huge sum did not intimidate the Coxcomb at all. He was, singlehandedly, offering his village, not only a mighty mansion which he named *Ngwene Mansion* but also a passable road.

It took one year for the construction of both the road and the mansion to be effected. And all this time Pa Kaloka's body was freezing in Switzerland. The villages thought that it was worth the trouble because the situation had made them have a good road and a glittering mansion, the type of building one finds only in the big cities. Their only regret was that Pa Kaloka had not lived to see the wonders of his vibrant son. Everything in preparation for the funeral was set. Invitations had been sent to different personalities. The Kitachi mansion had forty rooms to accommodate the cream of guests. Ten other neighbouring houses had been renovated and a giant power generating plant had been installed. Kitachi was going to have non-stop electricity supply two days before the arrival of the corpse and one week after the burial. Food and drinks were going to be served free of charge. Twenty ekpe houses in the region were invited to receive the corpse at the international airport and to ride in a convoy to Kitachi. So on the day of the arrival of Pa kaloka's corpse the airport was flooded by an array of sesekus in their traditional regalia, each leading the members of his ekpe house. It was a colourful spectacle to watch – men of different heights and shapes, wearing white long-sleeved shirts and overflowing loincloths of expensive wax, lace or velvet material. On their heads were red woollen caps that folded forward, backward or sideward depending on the caprice of the wearer. Every cap was adorned with a feather or more. Mr Brown Kaloka, the Coxcomb had made sure a land cruiser had been hired for each of them and a bus for each group. When the plane carrying the corpse landed, the ekpe chiefs were on hand to receive it. After a series of rituals and songs, they whisked the coffin to a waiting hearse. The hearse was placed in the middle of a convoy that comprised all types of big cars including Hummer jeeps and Bentleys. It was a slow drive across the city, taking as many as five hours. By the time the convoy had gone past the city, a stop was made at the banks of the river that had sliced the country into two. Every member of the convoy was served with a dinner pack including wine. They ate, drank and the *ekpe* group entertained with a dance. At the end of the entertainment, the convoy set off and drove throughout the night. It arrived at Kitachi at five o'clock in the morning. The village was all lit up by a giant generating plant. Coxcomb had made sure that the lack of electricity in his village should not be a setback during his father's funeral. Everything had gone well. All the cars braved the difficult terrain and got to the village. It was the first time the villagers saw such a great number of vehicles and what type? The type used by celebrities. They all wished the dead could witness their own funeral. The organisation was impeccable. Hostesses of all shapes had been recruited for the pleasure of the invitees. Catering conglomerates had been hired to ensure the comfort of everyone who had come for the funeral. Usually, the *ekpe* people do not allow the exposure of the corpse of an *ekpe* chief to public glare but this time the rules had been bent. The corpse had been laid in a gallery in the Ngwene Mansion and the guests, according to their ranking in society had to walk past in a single file. It was another wonder that the *ekpe* people had left their late chief to be dressed in a suit. People expected him to have been dressed in a most exquisite *ekpe* regalia. It must be another case of where the rule had been bent. After the viewing of the corpse a group of professional mourners were

invited in to mourn the fallen hero. It was the *ekini* who
started it all. After a protracted shout he went and broke
down besides the coffin which was adorned with gold. He
wept and wept and then spontaneously the mourners took
over, drowning his voice. The women, a hundred of them,
wailed in song, tumbled and somersaulted all over the place,
getting up and performing some sort of acrobatic dance. It
was like pandemonium had been let loose. A lot of the guests
found the spectacle so interesting that they started
applauding gleefully, as if they were in some cultural
jamboree. This went on for forty minutes, after which the
mgbe drums resounded and the graceful dance of ekpe took
over the show. They danced for about two hours and then
retired to the hall allocated for them. There, they feasted
and conducted their rituals. Out in the gallery chairs were
brought out and an altar was put in place. It was time for a
requiem mass. It was ecumenical in nature as it was presided
at by two prophets of Pentecostal churches, one archbishop
of the Roman Catholic Church and another of the Anglican
Church, one moderator of the Presbyterian Church, a
prominent pastor of the Baptist church and an Imam of the
Islamic movement. It was a wonder how the service went
on so smoothly, every clergy man taking a turn in saying
something about the salvation of the dead man. Some of
the ekpe people and even their chiefs joined the church
service. At the end of the service, eulogy after eulogy was
said and finally the burial took place at a grave that had
been built at the east end of the gallery. The grave had been
lavishly decorated with marble. At sunset Pa Kaloka was
lowered into it. Unfortunately, it caused laughter when the
thoughtless pastor on performing the dust-to-dust ritual
started scratching the marble around him in an effort to get
some soil. The flap of the grave was finally covered and
just before mourners started leaving, a glittering Silver
coated Mercedes Benz 600 was driving slowly to the grave.

It attracted every one's attention and they were expectant of what-next. It drove onto the grave and each wheel stood on each of the four corners of the grave. The driver came out of the car well-dressed in a royal chauffeur suit, bowed and stepped aside. Suddenly, the coxcomb in his characteristic peacock manner took the microphone and called for every one's attention. "Dear mourners, thank you for coming to join me in burying my beloved father. As you can see, he was the pearl of my life but he never had an opportunity to drive in his own car. So the best I can do for him is offer him one. This glittering car is my gift to him. It will remain here permanently on his grave, in testimony that even though he had died unable to buy a car he has left behind a son who can buy as many as a hundred. Once again thank you all for coming. My father has been a man of peace, so there's no doubt you'll all return peacefully."

Every one moved away dumbfounded, wondering at such arrogant show of wealth. Those who knew much about *ekpe* wondered at the seriousness of the institution. The burial place of an *ekpe* chief is usually a well guarded secret but this time around everyone saw the corpse of one being lowered in a grave not even by other ekpe chiefs but by clergymen. Again the laws are subject to bending provided the propensity to pay fines is high enough. Among the many people who went away wondering at the arrogance of the wealth of the Coxcomb was his boss. On his part Coxcomb was very satisfied that he had given his father not only a befitting burial but a historic one. He felt very much at ease with himself, silently congratulating himself like the legendary lizard that it would take Kitachi another thousand years to have anyone buried like pa Kaloka. The Coxcomb was pre-emptive of the fact that his own children would not be able to give him a burial of that magnitude.

One week after he had returned to the city, his boss invited him to his office. He thought it was for a friendly chat because two days after his return, he had gone to thank him for having honoured the invitation to his village. He had taken along a fat envelope to impress him. He had accepted his envelope with a smile. So when he knocked and entered, his boss was busy with some files in front of him. He however took up his head and showed the Coxcomb a seat on one of the office sofas. When he had finished he walked up to meet the Coxcomb:

"How are you doing Mr Kaloka," said the boss.

"Very fine. Having finally buried the old man. It's such a big relief," said the Coxcomb.

"It surely is. It's not easy retaining a corpse for over one year. And by the way I didn't know there could be heaven in the middle of a jungle," the boss said light heartedly.

"Heaven in the midst of a jungle. What do you mean boss?"

"I'm talking about Kitachi. It's heaven in a jungle."

"Oh thank you boss. It's the least I could do for a village that has my umbilical cord buried somewhere in its backyard," the Coxcomb said proudly.

"In my opinion, the display of wealth was grossly exaggerated. Come to think of it, did you need to place a Mercedes 600 on your father's grave?"

"Oh yes, boss. My father deserved it, considering the sacrifice he had made to bring me up."

"True, he sacrificed for you and not for himself. That's why it's a sacrifice. He's played his role and gone. So you had better sacrifice for others not for him."

"But boss, you've just talked about heaven in jungle. Have I not provided that heaven for the people of Kitachi?"

"Of course you have, but it's thanks to your father's funeral."

This statement embarrassed Brown Kaloka and it kept him thinking for some time. It reminded him that he had to keep his father's corpse in a cooler for over a year in order to get that heaven realised.

"Well boss, every sacrifice impinges on a motivation. My father's death was a motivation."

"Understood but you needn't exaggerate. Imagine that the bigger boss was there. I mean the Minister. Do you think he would have been impressed?"

"Impressed! Why not? The occasion was meant to impress every single person in attendance."

"I see. But I'm not sure the boss would have been happy about such lavish expenditure and I'm sorry to say much of it was wasteful. I would be surprised if there weren't any undercover security people around the place."

"I don't care a damn. I've been taking care of the Minister in my own way. He's my pal if you didn't know. He didn't come for the occasion because of some official exigencies. So boss, you need not lose any sleep over this matter."

"All right Brown, I do understand you. Only I thought I should caution you. In everything one does as a public servant, they have to be very careful. Have a nice day."

"I do appreciate your concern boss. Do have a nice day too," the Coxcomb said getting out of his chair.

Six months later, there were appointments in the Ministry of Finance. Brown Kaloka the Coxcomb had been waiting to be retained in his position or moved to an even juicier one. He was very satisfied with the ground work he had carried out. So when the appointments were being read on the radio after the five p.m. news, he was glued to the radio set in his office. It was a tortuous exercise as a very long list of appointees had to be listened to. It went on and on until it finally got to the Department of customs. Brown kaloka took a deep breath and waited nervously. The lists kept coming on and finally he heard a name that replaced him at his present position. The first wave of anxiety was over and he had to wait for his new position. He waited again for ten agonizing minutes and finally his name came up. He had been appointed as a Technical Adviser in the Ministry. When that wave of anxiety subsided, he wondered and wondered what had happened to him. Was the position of Technical Adviser not meant for old men and of course women who were near retirement? What would a young dynamic officer like him be doing as a technical adviser? He concluded that something had gone wrong somewhere. A week after the appointments had been read, he handed over to his successor and then moved to the ministry to assume his new function. It was then that the sad realities of being a public servant began to dawn on him. A lot of money that he had accumulated in a very short time had been used up for the funeral. His bank account still had a whooping half a billion francs. But he was not the type of man who would want to cut down on his lifestyle. So month after month the account was dwindling. His monthly salary seemed like pocket allowance for a spoilt secondary school child. He had two children in a private elementary school in England and he spent two million francs monthly on the children. Being a Coxcomb, his taste of a wife had driven him to the type of woman whom it takes a fortune to keep. He needed at least a million francs monthly to run his home. He decided he would maintain his lifestyle in the hope that a juicy appointment will not take long in coming. And so his savings began to dwindle. It took him five years to realise that his five hundred million francs fortune had dwindled to fifty million. One of the first victims of this economic crunch was Kitachi. The power generating station was shut down and Kitachi was deprived of electricity. People who had used their cocoa money to buy TV sets and even refrigerators were regretting because they could no longer use them. It was a wonder to them that their illustrious son had suddenly become incapable of keeping alive the power generating plant, especially because it lit the *Ngwene Mansion* and the entire compound at night. It was difficult for them to understand but when they saw that the workers who had been employed to take care of the mansion had been leaving one after another, they began to understand. When the last labourer left, the beautiful lawns of the mansion were invaded by wild grass and soon the building itself started to feel the strain of abandonment. Coxcomb himself hardly came round to supervise his investments. Many times he had been tempted to return and take away the Mercedes 600 he had offered his late father but he could not swallow his pride to do such a thing. However, one day he got in a financial wrangle with his dear wife:

"Now tell me Brown, what's a several-millions-worth car doing on your father's tomb, when we are in dire need of money. The children in England need their fees to be paid. I personally need to travel with them to Disneyland in summer. You've got to do something about it. However, if you can afford the money for their fees and the trip then there'd be no problem. But I doubt it very much. From the way things are going, I doubt it."

"So what are suggesting?" Brown asked doubtfully.

"Go and collect it and put it on sale," she said.

"Put it on sale! That's the last thing I'll do. Sell something that I had honoured my father with posthumously." Brown said clenching his fist.

"In that case you'll cough out the money for my needs and those of your children, who unfortunately are out there in the cold."

"If it's cold out there, then we better bring them back home. It will even be cheaper for us," Brown said feeling relieved.

"What? Bring my children to this country? You must be made to even think of such a thing. Tell me the name of anyone worth the salt in this country whose child is being educated here? Besides, these are children whose basic education was taken care of in Europe and because you have suddenly become poor you want them to come here and be frustrated for life? No not my child. Not when I'm alive," she said.

"My dear I was simply reacting to your observation that the children were out there in the cold," Brown said apologetically.

"Well that's not the type of cold I meant," she said walking away.

Brown Kaloka leaned back and thought seriously about how singlehandedly he had landed himself into such a frying pan. He wondered what the hell made him send his children to England whereas he himself had had his education at home in worse conditions. He also wondered what madness got into him to choose a diplomat's daughter for a wife. Her thinking and behaviour were so superficial. All she thinks about is spending money, never bothering how it comes about. His available cash was flying off so fast and he seemed to move further and further away from a position that would put him back on his feet. Brown Kaloka, the Coxcomb wondered and wondered until he fell asleep on the couch.

When he got up the following morning, it was to prepare to go to work. That drudgery of a job. A Technical Adviser who's got almost nothing to do. A Technical Adviser who's never been invited into the Minister's office. "What a life!" Brown exclaimed and went to the bathroom.

When he returned home that day he decided he would travel to Kitachi to collect the Mercedes 600. He had decided to swallow his pride, get it out of Kitachi and advertise it for sale. He hoped that the car would still be in perfect condition. It had not been used and it had been standing on marble in a gallery. He hired a mechanic who was also a driver to go along with him. It was a very rough drive to the village as it was during the wet season. Brown Kaloka was obliged to take public transport, something he had not done for a very long time. Even though he had paid for four seats that would take him and his hired driver, the stress of the journey was still enormous. The road had degraded a lot. It was slippery, muddy and with deep gullies. They managed to get there but it was after dusk. To get into the mansion, they needed flashlights. It was pitch darkness around the *Ngwene Mansion.* The Coxcomb did not bother to go to the other end of the village, where the chief lived. Not many people were aware of his presence, especially as it had not been heralded by at least a big four-wheel drive car. He saw how things had depreciated at the mansion. The grass had grown wild, some of it creeping into the mansion. He simply shook his head sadly. He got a room opened for the driver and another for himself. They both used their flashlights to deal with the darkness. They got up very early and worked on the Mercedes car and by half past seven the mechanic-driver was behind the steering wheel and they left the village. Some of the villagers who had realised what was happening and had come to witness it watched in shame at what they saw. They thought it was a dishonour for a dead man's tomb to be interfered with without any traditional rites. Besides, the chief of the village had not even been notified. The car drove on and on, getting stuck in very muddy spots of the road. And then it got to a slippery slope. By the time the time the driver knew what was happening, the car was sliding dangerously downhill. He wheeled it to the left and it swerved and plunged into a somersault, which went on and on deep down a valley. Fortunately the occupants had on their seatbelts, which kept them strapped to their seats. When the somersaults stopped, the victims were glad they were still alive. They managed to un-strap themselves and got out of the ruined limousine. They were on their buttocks for a full thirty minutes. Then they started the climb from down below. The Coxcomb had been taken unawares. He had never trained for an activity as strenuous as climbing up a near cliff. It took them two hours to finally get back to main road. It was a wonder they managed to do it at all. They sat at the side of the road waiting to be rescued. After another hour, rescue came. A goods only lorry was going to the nearest town. When the driver saw them, they were a very sorry sight. The motor-boy bundled both of them at the back of the lorry, among the bags of cocoa and coffee. By the time they got to the nearest health centre, the men had passed out. An hour later, the driver came round and realised that they were at a health centre. He watched Brown Kaloka still lying and breathing gently. The nurses had been working hard to get them reanimated and so they were very hopeful when the driver came round. An hour later, he rolled his eyes from side to side, wondering where he was. The mechanic-driver understood and said:

"We are at a health Centre."

"Health Centre! What happened?" the Coxcomb asked.

"We drove down a deep valley," the driver said.

"Ah, I remember. I remember the car is wrecked. Thank God we didn't get wrecked with it," the Coxcomb said optimistically.

"I'm glad to hear that. I thought you were going to miss the car so much," said the driver.

"I'm gradually learning not to miss anything. I wonder if I had died in the accident any of my many things would have missed me. I now understand that things don't actually matter. You saw the mansion in the village. You can't imagine how much it cost me, can you?"

"No way, I can't. But it has to be an enormous amount of money."

"It's a staggering amount which I'm not sure I'll ever have again, even if I spend the rest of my life making nothing but money. Come to think of it, I got that money in the twinkling of an eye. At that time it was good and I felt great. Then it started weighing on me and I started crumbling under the weight, desperately seeking redemption. That car was going to replenish my pockets, now it's been wrecked down the valley. I've learnt not to wreck myself when the things I acquire get wrecked. They are only things which should be no bother. And invariably money that acquires them shouldn't be much of a bother. I had become too intimate with money but thanks be to God Almighty that this intimacy hasn't ended in fatality. I can now see clearly that I was sliding dangerously into gaining an entire world of wealth at the expense of my true life."

Three days later, Brown Kaloka the Coxcomb and his driver were discharged from the village health centre. Fortunately for them, their rescuers had been kind-hearted enough not to have mugged them in their misery.

The Phoney Phone Call

L ike every responsible citizen, I left my home one morning at quarter past seven in the morning. Just a few minutes before half past seven I was already seated in my office ready for the day's work. After examining my day's planning I started work in earnest. At ten o'clock my secretary entered to inform me I had a phone call from the state house.

"A call from the state house," I muttered. "Pass it on" I requested.

"Hello, Tim here, Tim Tabufo"

"Hello Dr Tabufo, I'm col. Zambo Zam of the state house security."

"I'm sorry, I've not heard that name before. What can I do for you?"

"It's what you can do for yourself doctor"

"In that case there's nothing to do."

"I'm sorry but it's urgent. The state house needs your CV and your party card."

"What for?"

"For your good."

"For my good? I don't understand. Something sinister must be going on. I'm very sure I haven't asked the state for anything and so I shouldn't expect anything that will be given me on the bases of my CV and party card. And by the way what party card are you asking for?"

"The People's Party of course."

"That's where you got it all wrong. I'm not a member of the people's party. So can you now leave me alone?"

"No, not when the Head of State needs you."

"What! The head of state needs me? Does he even know me?"

"Yes, he knows you very well and he wants you to help him get this country out of the hopeless mess it has got itself into. The Head of State is counting so much on your cooperation."

"You say, you're colonel who?"

"Zambo Zam, doctor."

"All right col. Zambo Zam. Thanks very much for the call. I'll call you back."

"I'll be patient in waiting."

When I put down the phone, I recalled the story of many a civil servants who had been conned into coughing out millions to ensure dream positions in government. There was this good friend who had received such a phone call requesting him to take temporary accommodation in a suite in a five-star hotel pending his appointment as prime minister. The Head of state was to meet him in his suite and discuss installation arrangements and other issues. Every day the con men came up with one story or another which made my friend to freely sign out cheques. By the time he knew he was being conned, he had spent everything he had as savings. Come to think of it, some of the people involved were actually linked to the state house.

I put down my head and thought hard. I wondered whether I should call the state house and inquire about Col. Zambo Zam. And if he was unknown, how would someone decide to use an institution like the state house to con people. This is tantamount to dragging state institutions in the mud. Has our level of corruption brought us this low? I wondered and kept wondering at the expense of what I had earlier planned to do. Then the phone rang.

"Dr Tim Tabufo," the caller inquired.

"Speaking."

"Well Dr Tabufo, I've just remembered that I didn't leave you a number to call back so I decided to call again. But all the same I should remind you about the seriousness of our previous discussion. The Head of State is very much aware that the state in its current state is rotten and to fix it he needs people like you."

"But Col. Zambo Zam, remember I don't belong to the party and you had said that one of the requirements for such considerations was a party card."

"Yes, I had said so but when a house is on fire, even an enemy can be called upon to help put it off. So this is an opportunity for you to serve your nation."

"All right Col Zam. I would have thought that you have up-to-date information about whoever you want to use at the state house. How come you're requesting me to send you my CV."

"It's for verification. We would want to compare the information we have and that which you send."

"I see your point"

"So how do I send it?"

"Use the following e-mail address: zamzam@yahoo.co.uk."

"I'm afraid this address is rather personal than institutional."

"It doesn't matter. As soon as the CV gets to me, it will be duly sent to the appropriate quarters. I'm expecting to have it in an hour's time."

"Well Col. Zambo, it's been nice talking to you. I've got work to do, bye."

When I put down the receiver I tried to concentrate on my work but I had lost the zeal. I thought I should send the CV but on second thoughts I decided it was not worth the trouble. These con men have had tremendous success with chicken hearted people who are desperate to jump at any available opportunity. I don't think I should join in such a dance. I took a break hoping that when I come back my zeal to work would have returned. Unfortunately, as soon as I sat down, the phone rang.

"Hello, Tim here. Whom am I talking to?"

"Col Zambo."

"You again!"

"Yes, me again. I've called because I haven't seen the CV yet."

"So don't expect to see it ever. I'm actually sick and tired of these pranks. If you're the colonel you purport to be, then you should have better things to occupy yourself with.

I'm not sure I want to be disturbed by any more of your phoney phone calls."

"My respects sir, I'm sorry doctor. I'm simply carrying out instructions. And being such a dependable soldier I'm condemned to carry out instructions to the last letter. This is the reason for my being so insistent."

"I'm not sure I'm in the mood to listen to anymore of this trash," I said putting down the receiver.

After a while, I thought I should not let this Zamzam man get away with such pranks. He might have conned so many people already and it was time someone stopped him. I was determined to be that someone. I sent the CV two hours after our last conversation. As soon as he received it, he called to acknowledge receipt and went further to arrange an appointment between me and the head of the state protocol. The meeting was to take place the following day in the lounge of Central Hotel. He too would be in attendance. He went ahead to request that I send him a hundred thousand francs, for the necessary logistics, through telephone credit transfer. When I got the message, I decided to sacrifice the money. I made some enquiries at the state house and then reported the matter to some highly placed persons at the state house and I was given a cover.

Prior to the time of the appointment, Col. Zambo Zam had asked me to describe what I would wear and to come along with five hundred thousand francs for the boss's champagne. I got dressed in a grey suit and at five p.m.

prompt I was at the lounge of Central hotel. I sat on a brown leather couch and five minutes later I was served a drink. I sipped my drink gently and by half past five someone walked up to me. He was smartly dressed in a light blue suit. His black pointed shoes had been meticulously polished as they shone with a reflection. He was about one metre seventy eight centimetres tall. Not a bad height for a soldier. He was dark with a broad forehead. He was in his late forties and he held a walkie talkie in his left hand. When he got close enough he began to speak:

"Good evening, Dr Tabufo"

"Good evening. I presume you're Col. Zambo Zam."

"You're right."

"My pleasure to meet you in person."

"My pleasure too.

"Well, Col Zambo, take a seat."

"Thank you. But things have to be snappy. The boss is in suite number 007. He must not be kept waiting."

"The boss. Who?"

"The one I had told you, you were going to meet. The Head of the state protocol. He would give you the initial briefing."

"Is he there at suite 007 right now?"

"What a question? I've just told you he's there and he's got no time to waste. So let's go."

"Wait a minute, the Head of the state protocol is a friend of mine and he's right now in New York on an official assignment. So I don't know what you're talking about."

Colonel Zambo Zam looked as embarrassed as an unmasked masquerade at a public square, in broad daylight. He pretended to make a call on his walkie talkie but he soon realized his game was up when security men in mufti closed in and whisked him off.

Tension on an Arrival

The first lady, in her usual munificence has been doing great for the depraved, especially children whom for no fault of theirs are the most vulnerable of humans. It was in this regard that her attention was turned to Griefland constituency. She had never set foot on this constituency although from time to time she heard about the suffering of the people who live there, especially when it came to roads. It was the constituency where the adage about roads bringing about development does not apply. People heard about Griefland only when elections were around the corner. The entire constituency was usually cut off from the rest of the country when the rains arrived. Unfortunately, the people have the tradition of taking back their dead home. So during these seasons when they are caught up by the rains, a lot of these persons end up being buried by the roadside. It was a blessing for anyone to die in the dry season, when in spite of the dust and deep gutters on the road, the corpse usually arrived at its resting place.

This had been a preoccupation of the first lady for a long time because she had hardly understood why after several decades of nationhood some parts of the country could still not be reached by road. She had confronted her husband on several occasions about this vexing issue but it had each time degenerated into a domestic squabble. She decided she would let sleeping dogs lie, and concentrate on the things she could do. One of the things she could do was the creation and building of schools for the underprivileged.

Griefland had been well noted for being underprivileged, so the first lady decided to take an interest in the place. First she sent a delegation there to carry out an analysis of the problems. Then she studied the report meticulously and decided she would create a school there. It would be a school for the fatherless child.

Schools for fatherless children had been a serious preoccupation of the first lady's. Even though it is easily claimed that mothers are the backbone of child education and development, experience has shown that the absence of a father in a home poses a very serious handicap. The scum of every community is usually dominated by fatherless children who are commonly referred to as *akwara pikin*. Appropriate education for them will obviously be a rescue and they will become useful citizens in a dependable citizenry. Besides, such schools will go a long way to reducing the number of street children. Such children are among the many people who have lost the will to live and have become dangerous to themselves and invariably the community. How else can it be explained that a young man will take the risk of attacking a young lady in broad daylight, just to get her cell phone, or kill a young tourist because he thinks the latter's camera may fetch him a few francs. Such children need the education that will enable them to understand that every human being can be proud and happy only when they earn what they have. The first lady had set out establishing such schools around chosen places in the country. Griefland had the luck to be known by her and so the constituency was eventually placed on the list of beneficiaries of her magnanimity.

Grieflanders received the news with much enthusiasm and naturally they drafted and sent a powerful motion of support to the first lady's husband, wishing him eternal life. Shortly after, a team was sent to Griefland to identify a location for the school. Unfortunately, the constituency is made up of several communities and it was difficult for them to agree on where the school should be located. Each village wanted the school, so after much wrangling four sites were agreed upon. It was left for the team to visit the sites and make a decision. The team had to go to each of the four sites. Members of each community had as a duty to work hard enough to impress the team so that their site be chosen. In which case, wherever the team went they were not only fed sumptuously but were also given gifts that included livestock. So by the time they had made their rounds, it was difficult to make good judgment.

Their stomachs were quite full and their hands too were full. It was a very fruitful mission for each member of the team. So in order to satisfy the people they decided that the school be located in Tarkamanda, the headquarters of the constituency. Two weeks after the team's report had been submitted; a call for tenders for the construction of the school was announced. The tender's board received twenty submissions, among which was that of HRH Chief Nfor Seseku Nyukechen I. Before the meeting of the board to consider the submissions, the chairman called Chief Nyukechen and drew his attention to an issue he considered pertinent.

"Chief are you aware that members of the board are not supposed to bid for this contract?"

"No, but why shouldn't they?"

"You amaze me chief. One can't be comfortably seated as a judge and at the same time nervously standing in the dock."

"I'm sorry I don't understand"

"Well chief, it's like this: If you have to score your own bid, there's no way you'll be objective."

"I see the point you're trying to make. In this case I'll opt to resign from the board. This contract is very important for me. I can't afford to lose it. So even as I quit the board, those of you who are there will surely cater for my interest."

"Yes, we shall but you'll have to change a few things. In order not to give the public the impression that you had resigned from the board in order to win the contract, it be in our interest to redo you submission in another name."

"You're right. You're a very smart person. I'll do just that," said chief Nyukechen.

So for the chief, it was no surprise that he had to execute the contract to build the *Griefland School for the Fatherless.* Two thirds of the money was made available so as to facilitate the construction. Besides, chief Nyukechen had been unable to raise any money to get the work started. He managed to use this first instalment to execute the entire contract. The school buildings did not reflect the architect's plan, nor were the materials used cost a third of the amount that had been allocated for them. The furniture and equipment were of very inferior quality. In spite of all these shortcomings, the reception committee approved of the work and the chief was paid the rest of his money. He used it to improve on his status by buying a Nissan X-trail luxurious four-wheel drive car. The chief could then measure up even with the representative of the constituency at the parliament. In the course of executing the contract, he had also engaged in refurbishment of his palace. So he could then boast a good house, a good car and a good savings account. He became more confident and of course arrogant. The school opened its doors the following academic year and had an enrolment of a hundred fatherless kids.

One cool evening, as the chief was enjoying a bottle of beer under a shed tree in his palace, he heard a piece of news that should please anyone from Griefland. Unfortunately, it made the beer in his mouth taste like the bile of a porcupine. The piece of news was that the first lady was going to visit Tarkamanda, the headquarters of Griefland. As soon as he digested what had been said, Chief Nyukechen poured out the stuff in his mouth, got up from his seat and walked away from the shade tree. He went into his room and lay on his bed in an attempt to relax. He wondered what must have prompted the first lady to think of visiting Griefland. "What will she think of the contract I have executed? If she insists on probity then I'll surely be a prisoner, my status of a chief notwithstanding. I must do something before it's too late. Fortunately, there are these timber exploitation companies. I'll have to do fast business with them," he concluded.

Chief Nyukechen immediately swung into action and sent someone to take an appointment, on his behalf, with the Manager of the Timber company.

Two days later the Manager was at the Chief's palace to keep the appointment.

"Here am I chief, very anxious to know what His Royal Highness requires of his humble servant," the Manager said seriously.

"Don't be ridiculous Mr eh Olabihi, you're no servant of mine," said the chief.

"Yes, I am. Everyone living or doing business within your chiefdom is your subject. And subjects are of course servants," the Manager said smiling.

"Okay, okay, whatever you say. To cut a long story short. We are expecting the visit of the first lady here in less than a month's time. And what this means is that the community must mobilise its material and financial resources to give her a rousing reception. And you know, you're the only viable economic operator I can count on."

"What exactly would you want me to do?"

"Good question. If the first lady is coming here, it is to inaugurate the School for fatherless children. This school should be given a wash-up before she arrives."

"But chief, the school has only recently been built and besides, someone had taken the contract to do that. That person should do the wash-up in view of the inauguration."

"To tell the truth, that person happens to be me. I carried out the construction of the school using very limited means and now I've got nothing left. I've got to count on you."

"Okay Chief, I do understand your worry."

"You had better do. So I'll take you to the site one of these days and make you familiar with what you've got to do exactly."

The meeting with Mr Olabibi was a great source of relief for chief Nyukechen. He had found in him someone who would likely bail him out of the tumultuous situation of a badly executed contract. He now had the entire community to rally for the reception of the first lady. He would work with the mayor, the parliamentarian and government officials of the constituency.

The mayor had been chosen to head the preparation committee. This committee was to ensure a hitch-free visit. The mayor, a short man with a proud walk was well known for his strictness and a high sense of justice and fairness. He was one who hated failure and so it was no coincidence that he had to head the committee.

In one of the meetings where economic operators were being identified, the mayor of Tarkamanda said:

"I think we should expect a lot of assistance from the timber company, they are the only big time economic operator in our constituency."

"That's true, but we have to be careful about not overworking a willing horse to death," said chief Nyukechen.

"How do you mean? Have we made any demands on them before?"the mayor asked.

"Yes of course, all these projects- markets, classrooms and even latrines."

"The projects are carried out using royalties from timber," said the mayor.

"Timber royalties are paid by the timber company. So they shouldn't be bothered with additional responsibilities," the chief concluded.

"I'm really taken aback by your reasoning. You know for sure that one of the conditions for exploitation was to pay royalties to the different communities just as they pay taxes to the government, which does not stop them from giving occasional help to the community in which the operate, when the need arises."

"Well, the need has arisen but we don't start by going a begging when we haven't mobilised our own resources yet. So I would advise that we go to the timber company only as a last resort," chief Nyukechen said persuasively.

The mayor looked doubtful as he looked at the parliamentarian for support and then the faces of the other participants at the meeting. No-one seemed ready to counter the argument of His royal highness. So he capitulated, letting things go the chief's way.

The population was therefore mobilised and each household in the entire constituency was levied a sum of five thousand francs. The internal and external elite were levied proportionately to their statuses, ranging from twenty thousand francs to five hundred thousand francs. Because it was the first time a personality of the calibre of the first lady was visiting Tarkamanda, everyone made an effort to pay their levy. The committee to oversee the success of the visit was meticulous in collecting and handling the funds. They were very transparent and the people trusted especially as it was headed by their mayor.

In carrying out his function, the mayor discovered that the timber company had taken up the responsibility of refurbishing the *School for the Fatherless*. The doors which had been made of warped wood had all been replaced. The flooring had been redone, using ceramic tiles and the walls painted with high quality paint. A solid fence was being built round the premises. On further investigation, he found out that the company was doing all that to gratify the chief.

He went straight to the palace to confront the chief:

"Your royal highness, I now understand why you were so bent on not getting the timber company involved in the preparations for this visit."

"Which visit are you talking about," the chief asked pretentiously.

"Don't be ridiculous, your highness. I mean the visit of the first lady."

"I see. But still I don't understand why you say I was bent on not getting the timber company involved."

"Chief you had insisted on us doing things for ourselves."

"Yes, of course but that was not to say that the company was not going to be involved."

"I've seen how you've involved them. To clean up the mess you did at the school in the name of executing a contract. Chief, were it not that you incarnate our traditional institution, which we respect so much I would have done something really terrible to you. The extent of your greed is taking unprecedented proportions. You must watch out, you are herding people not sheep."

Before the chief could say anything, he had already walked out. Chief Nyukechen became very tense and felt very uncomfortable. What if these revelations are made known to the first lady, then he would be finished. He decided to take a low profile as the rest of the preparations to receive the first lady progressed. Coincidentally, the chairman of the preparation committee had sidelined him. Tarkamanda had become as busy as a hive. Visitors poured in on a daily basis and they had to be taken care of. Farmers stopped going to their farms in order to participate in clean up campaigns, which had become a daily occurrence. The bumpy earth roads were being repaired manually. So it was a great relief for everyone when the day of the visit finally came round, it was a great for Tarkamandans and the entire Griefland.

People had lined the roads which had been decorated with yellow palm fronds and other colourful plants. As they waited, a helicopter appeared from the clouds and descended towards the playground of the public primary school. It circled the playground a couple of times and then landed. It was the first lady's helicopter. She had taken everyone by surprise, including government officials who had come to receive her. The situation caused a stir as people had to hurry to the play ground to welcome the first lady. Chief Nyukechen got very tense wondering why the first had decided to take everyone by surprise. Had she come to wage a war or to reconcile the people with their leadership. Had she already got information about his mishandling of the contract and had come to teach him a lesson? Chief Nyukechen kept wondering and getting more and more uneasy. The first lady had to stay in the aircraft for a while to enable protocol to put things in order. The security officials, administration and population eventually got to the makeshift airport. She descended from the craft and like the Roman Catholic Pope, decided to prostrate and kiss the ground. Everyone was amazed as she had never done such a thing before, not even on the day of her triumphal return to her native village. Chief Nyukechen attributed the gesture as a cover up of the weakness of the preparation committee that has not prepared a young girl to offer her a bouquet of flowers on arrival. It was a terrible mistake and the chief was determined to point it out to the mayor who was the chairman of the committee.

"What happened to the flower girl Mr Mayor?" chief Nyukechen asked as soon as he got close to the mayor.

"Which flower girl, thief?"

"What did you just say?"

"I said which flower girl, chief?"

"Oh, I thought you had said something else. Well, the girl who was supposed to present flowers to the first lady as soon as she arrived."

115

"You noticed the scenario changed suddenly. There's no time to harp on trivialities, excuse me," the mayor said and left to attend to more important things.

Chief Nyukechen, looking really worried, tried hard to read the first lady's mind from her countenance but could not be sure of the results. They had moved to the grounds of the school as they went round visiting the premises, the first lady was visibly impressed. The painting was good, the tiles quite appealing and the decoration wonderful. In spite of this the chief still felt uneasy. He was anxiously waiting for the first lady's speech, so when the moment came his heart was in his mouth. He kept expecting what he wanted to hear until at the tail end of the speech when the first lady pronounced the words: "this school is my precious gift to the people of Tarkamanda and Griefland constituency as a whole. I'm well pleased with the premises and I do hope it is being put in good use. It is my desire that one day, Griefland will change its name into Gloryland," the first lady said enthusiastically amidst thunderous applause. After the speech, the ritual of cutting the tape was effected and then the mood at Tarkamanda turned festive. By the time the population waved to the glittering helicopter which had on board the first lady, a wave of extreme relief swept through the minds of the likes of His Royal Highness Seseku Chief Nfor Nyukechen the first of Tarkamanda.

The following day, the mayor met the chief at the evaluation meeting and said:

"Chief I know how you feel."

"How do I feel my dear mayor?"

"All conquering, my dear chief, but remember, timber and timber companies are not perennial."

"How do you mean?"

"Reflect better chief and you're know what I mean" the mayor said and walked away.